# Thirty at Thirty

LIBRARY AND ARCHIVES CANADA CATALOGUING IN PUBLICATION

Thirty at thirty : an anthology of prose and poetry celebrating 30 years of Ottawa Independent Writers / edited by Robert Barclay.

ISBN 978-0-920987-11-7 (paperback)

1. Short stories, Canadian (English)--Ontario--Ottawa.
2. Canadian fiction (English)--21st century. 3. Canadian poetry (English)--Ontario--Ottawa. 4. Canadian poetry (English)--21st century. I. Barclay, R. L. (Robert L.), editor II. Ottawa Independent Writers, issuing body

PS8257.O88T45 2016    C813'.010971384    C2016-905715-1

Copyrights ©
2016 Ottawa Independent Writers
Cover design: Magdalene Carson, New Leaf Publication Design

All rights reserved. Except for use in any review or critical article, the reproduction or use of this work, in whole or in part, in any form by any electronic, mechanical or other means—including xerography, photocopying and recording—or in any information or storage retrieval system, is forbidden without express permission of the publisher and the contributors.

Published by
OTTAWA INDEPENDENT WRITERS
www.oiw.com

# Thirty at Thirty

## An Anthology of Prose and Poetry Celebrating 30 Years of Ottawa Independent Writers

## Acknowledgements

The Board of Directors of OIW would like to acknowledge the editorial assistance of Benoit Chartier, Meghan Negrijn and Alex Robinson, and Magdalene Carson for the cover design. A project of this scope would be impossible without the enthusiastic participation of all our members, so we are grateful to those who submitted their works for inclusion in this volume.

Robert Barclay
September 2016

## Foreword

It's been 30 years since a disparate group of Ottawa writers decided it was time to get together. The initiators included Claire Harrison, Clive Doucet, Blaine Marchand, Colin Morton, Margot Andresen, Anne Stephenson, Don Cummer, Donna Neff, Dinah Shields, Roy MacSkimming, and a few others. I joined after they had got the ball rolling. And roll it did! By 1990 we had hundreds of members, had organized a successful conference, and had published many newsletters and several anthologies.

OIW members have always represented the complete range of writing: novelists (in many genres), poets, speechwriters, historians, journalists, essayists... and this 30th anniversary anthology shows the same spectrum. There continues to be a great deal of talent in OIW; some writers are beginners, others have years of writing experience, and some are beginning writers with years of experience in other fields.

I have read every story, essay and poem in here, and I heartily recommend them to you. You are sure to find a few—or many—that speak to you.

Barb Collishaw
September 2016

# Table of Contents

Norm Rosolen, *A Loon, a Bear and a Dog* .......... 1
Gladys Galay, *Snow Day* ...................... 7
Silvia Alfaro, *Living My Dreams* .............. 13
Jessica Clarke, *A Mother's Choice* ............ 17
Keith Newton, *A Nice Cup of Tea* .............. 23
Majid Kafai, *About Poetry* .................... 27
Keith Newton, *Oh Brother!* .................... 31
Qais Ghanem, *Message to Aylan* ................ 33
Laurie Stewart, *The Soul Eggs* ................ 35
Maggie Taylor, *A Little Harmless Flirtation* .......... 41
Neven Humphrey, *A Letter from Mrs Beezie Boddy* .... 53
Norm Rosolen, *The Writer* ..................... 57
Raeanne G. Roy, *The Solarium* ................. 61
Benoit Chartier, *Native* ...................... 67
Rem Westland, *Thanks for Your Service* ........ 71
Ian Prattis, *Vietnam War Memorial* ............ 77
Susan Taylor Meehan, *Today I Took Up Running* .... 79
Barbara Florio Graham, *Hero* .................. 83
Robert Barclay, *The Little Drummer* ........... 89
Norm Rosolen, *Welly* .......................... 91
Hazel Johnson, *Hawai'i: A Different Perspective* ....... 95
Ian Prattis, *Dawson's Desert Legacy* .......... 101
Peggy Lehmann, *The Message of the Rose* ....... 105
Molly O'Connor, *Bragging Rights* .............. 111
Raymond D. Tremblay, *The White Rose* .......... 115
Mary Ellen Kot, *Egg Thief* .................... 117
Robert Barclay, *There's a Short Story Here* ........ 121
Susan Taylor Meehan, *The Year of Not Speaking* .... 123
Benoit Chartier, *Extras* ...................... 129
Susan Jennings, *Eleanor Does Not Camp* ........ 133
Biographies of the Contributors ................ 141

# A Loon, a Bear and a Dog
## Norm Rosolen

*I* wake out of a deep sleep and find I'm lying on a hospital bed. Then the curtain opens, and a beautiful woman framed by a halo pokes her head in.

"Are you an angel?" I say.

"Good morning Bob. Glad to see you're awake. I'm definitely not an angel. I'm Judy, and you're a guest of the North Bay Health Centre. You've been here for two days. In a coma. You're very lucky considering. Some bear bites, lost blood and a concussion. But nothing's broken and there's hardly a scratch to that pretty face of yours." Judy winks and straightens the bedsheet across my chest.

"My head's bursting Judy. I've got a brain tumour, and I'm sore all over."

"Getting whacked by a bear explains why you're sore all over. And we've got some pills for that head of yours courtesy of your friend Amy and your doctor." Judy feeds me three pills and some water. "Amy's in a motel near here. I'll call her cell."

She leaves; the pills take over, and I doze.

Next thing I know Amy jolts me awake. She hugs me and sobs kind of piteously. It's nice to be wanted, so I don't tell her she's hurting me. Then she cradles my head in her hands and we kiss, which doesn't hurt at all. Then she stands back and wipes her eyes with her sleeve. She looks bleary and reproachful but gorgeous nonetheless.

"You sod. Why do have to do everything the hard way? Do you have any idea what happened?"

"A bear tried to eat me."

"Serves you right. I came home from work, and there was your stupid note. You said you needed to sort things out." She snuffles. "Why?"

"Maybe because I'm dying?"

She crosses her arms and raises her voice a touch. "You took off before we got the biopsy results. Why didn't you wait? Why didn't you talk to me? Or at least go somewhere where I could call you?"

I hunker under my bed sheet as far as I can. "I couldn't. Look, it's the way I am. I'm sorry but I needed to breathe, get away from it. And I figured if I told you, you'd talk me out of it. So I took off for Temagami."

Amy's voice escalates another notch. "Well, did you get away from it?"

"Maybe a bit. No, not really."

"See. You should've waited. Your doctor said to tell you congratulations on surviving, and she's got good news. Your tumour's benign. They can get rid of it. Your headaches and hallucinations will be gone." Amy starts crying again.

What!? My heart pounds and my throat constricts. I'm going to live, be normal. A tear starts to well up, but I fight it off. "It's okay sweetheart. I survived, and I'm going to get better. I'll get the operation, and we can go somewhere. Take a holiday."

Angry, happy, sad, mixed-up, Amy wipes away tears with her sleeve. "A holiday? Is that all you can say?"

I'm confused. What should I say? "How's Maggie?"

Amy sighs and lightens up. "What am I going to do with you? I've got her. She's fine."

"Thank God."

Amy's perplexed smile morphs into a proud, happy one. Her chest puffs out.

"Actually, Maggie's a national hero," she says. "Made the news everywhere in Canada and internationally too. Because it was a dog story. One of the Parks people did a video with her cell phone of Maggie fighting the bear. It's on YouTube. Went viral."

I'm stunned. "Parks people? Maggie fighting the bear?" Maggie, who'd jump into my arms if a chihuahua looked at her cross-eyed, fought the bear?

Amy shoots me her superior female look. "You'd be bear poop if Maggie hadn't kept nipping at that bear and making it forget about you for a few seconds between bites. You were lucky there was a Parks boat around the corner checking out campsites. They found you and chased the bear away."

I sigh. "It's crazy, Amy. I can remember every detail up to the attack. Like a movie."

"You have a terrible memory." She looks doubtful.
"Not for that day."

It's our sixth day out when the bear tries to eat me. It starts out ordinary enough. Great weather, easy paddling, beautiful scenery. We're going down Sucker Gut Lake and Maggie's curled up on the floor of the canoe, snoozing away, yipping at some dream-rabbit, and I'm thinking about stuff. You know, like dying. Then it's noon so I say, "Maggie, wakey, wakey."

She looks up at me and says, "About time. It's hot down here." She has a really nice voice, kind of smoky, like Lauren Bacall in one of those 1940s movies. I've had her for five years, and I know she's smart, but not that smart.

"Maggie, how'd you learn to talk?"

She stands and yawns. "Never had the need before. But seeing how things are going. You know."

"Doc said I've got six, maybe eight months. But you'll be fine. Amy's going to look after you."

"Don't talk like that," she says. "Enjoy the day. Blue sky and those puffy little clouds. And eating always picks you up. Losing a few pounds wouldn't hurt either."

I grumble and turn the canoe towards shore. A loon with two chicks swims into view. They dive under us, and I can see them swimming a couple of feet down. They surface just in front and I stop paddling.

"Whoo are youu?" the mother loon says. There's a trill in her voice.

"I'm Bob, I think." Maggie pokes her head over the gunnels. "And this is Maggie. Whoo are youu?"

"Loraa. Loraa Loonn. Swimm withh uss."

"We're stopping for lunch. We'll join you later."

Amy interrupts. "A loon with two babies?"

"Yeah. Never hear of a talking loon before?"

"Uh, no. Go on with it," says Amy. "I'll explain when you finish."

Anyway, I land the canoe next to a large meadow, get some food and start to climb the bank. Then I almost fall on my face when

I hear a deep, nasal voice.

"Hey, what're you doin' here?"

It's a moose. Huge rack of antlers, grim serious mouth. Not good. I'd been chased by moose twice before. But this one reminds me of the comedian Rodney Dangerfield, so I stifle a laugh.

"We stopped for lunch," I say.

"Go away. We're having a party. Humans not allowed."

"I'm dying. Maybe that could qualify me."

The moose looks up and thinks for maybe 30 seconds. "Okay. You two can watch. But stay still and be quiet, otherwise you'll spoil it."

Spoil what? I sit myself against the trunk of a huge pine. Maggie puts her head on my lap. She's shivering. I take it she's a bit nervous. That's her collie nature.

Then all these animals come from nowhere and scatter themselves around. There's everything from wolves to chipmunks and every kind of bird. Next I hear, "Whoo, hoo, hooo," from my friends on the lake. With all the animal sounds going on it's like listening to a loony tunes cartoon show, but they're real enough. I see their scars, ragged fur and wary eyes.

The moose says, "Calm down, calm down." The animals go real quiet. He stares at each of them like he's the conductor of an orchestra. When he figures he's got their attention he nods.

The different animal voices rise and mingle into one perfect harmony and it's really mystical. I feel some kind of euphoria like I'm on drugs only better. Then I'm floating in outer space like an astronaut. There's star fields, auroras and planets, flickering, blinking, colourful in the background. I do the breast stroke and move right along.

We're lost for the longest time and no time at all, and I feel all this joy and I'm totally happy. It seems like I'm connected to everybody and everything in the universe, and I get this sense of really deep caring; love I guess. Like I'm God or Jesus or something. The Force is with me. You know, like *Star Wars*.

Then the music stops and I'm back under the tree, discombobulated, and pissed it's over.

Maggie nudges me. "We better move," she says, and I see why.

This huge black bear rumbles into the clearing, and all the animals take off. Maggie and I stand and back towards our canoe, not too fast. That's where my bear spray is. Maggie lets the F-word slip. I'm not going to correct her.

The bear has glassy, empty eyes and his mouth is twisted into a toothy, wicked grin like a boss I once had. Then he sits on his ass, crosses his arms and speaks.

"Well, what have we got here?" His voice is a slithering baritone, menacing and evil. "What makes you think that you can invade my territory and do whatever you want, you piddling excuses for animals?" He spits out 'piddling' like it's the worst thing in the world.

We almost get to the canoe, and I think we're okay when the bugger is on me so fast. He's a black blur, and has really bad breath. The smell almost makes me gag, except the pain takes most of my attention. Then I tuck myself into a ball, because I remember that's what you're supposed to do.

And then nothing. I guess I'm out, and Maggie saves me, so I'm told. And the Parks folks too.

Amy doesn't say anything, but now she's wired.

"There's more," she says. "You know when you said you talked to the loon. Something weird happened when you got attacked. A loon with two babies came out of nowhere and went crazy right in front of the Parks boat. She was kind of dancing on the water, flapping her wings, so they followed her. She led them straight to you."

"Whaa?"

"Please don't say it was the same loon."

"Lora," I say. "Loraa Loonn."

"Come on. That was an hallucination. Some kind of weird coincidence."

"Natives say the loon can open new realities and help make our wishes come true."

"Really?" She sounds very skeptical.

"Yeah, just wasn't my time to go."

"There's something else." She looks at me expectantly.

"Yeah?"

"I'm pregnant. Two months. My obstetrician says it's twins."

My head starts to spin. I want to say 'Who's the father?' or 'Why'd you hold back', but I know the answers. Eventually I figure it out. "You'll make a great mother."

"And you're going to be a great father."

"If they're girls, I'd like us to name them Margaret and Laura," I say.

Amy smiles sweetly and says, "Hmm. After a dog and a loon, eh? Maybe not," and kisses me on the forehead like I'm a particularly dumb child.

# Snow Day
## Gladys Galay

January 4th 2015, 6:15 a.m. I went out after the storm to shovel the snow from my walkway and my parking space, and to clean off my car. So early on a Sunday I was all alone. The new snow added six inches to the existing drifts around the condos. It was slow going as the freezing rain left an ice crust on the snow. After clearing my walkway, I leaned into the snow shovel and pushed a narrow path down the public sidewalk to the parking lot.

In spite of the dark this time of year, the floodlights on the side of the building lit the lot up like noon. Between most cars the snow drifts were more than a foot. I approached my space and, oh joy, it was over two feet deep on the left between my car and my neighbour's. Great.

I didn't want to deal with it so I started clearing the right side. Finally the space was clean. I pushed the snow off the car windows onto the left side, entered the passenger door and slid across to the driver's seat. Starting the car, I drove it slowly out of the snow bank and parked beside the refuse bins to clean the rest of it. I would deal with the huge snow drift later.

I was hoping one of the young men who worked for the condo complex would magically appear with a snow blower to clean it for me. I hoped it would be Andy. He was cute and always up for helping the women, if you catch my drift! Although I never took advantage of the offer, I heard others were more than happy to supplement a young man's income. The condo management company was known to be stingy.

It was strange no one was out working. I could not hear a motor anywhere.

6:55 a.m. Finally the car was clean of every speck and it was certain no Prince Charming was coming to my rescue. There was nothing for me to do but tackle the drift left in my parking space.

The snow was higher against my neighbour's car and far too much to push in any one direction. The only way was to start in the middle of the drift; pushing half back onto the sidewalk and half forward into the middle of the lot.

Turning the shovel sideways, I used the edge to break through the ice on top of the drift. It broke apart in sheets that slid towards my feet. The snow beneath clung to its shape. I needed to clear at least two feet of space in the middle to provide leverage for the push in either direction. The clean space behind me would be sacrificed but there was no alternative. I pushed the shovel into the top third of the drift and flung the snow behind me. Turning back I noticed a dark shadow beneath the snow in the space I just created.

"What is that?" Carefully this time, I cleaned a small space in the snow to examine what was beneath it; a quilted jacket? Clothes? A pile of clothes? Why would someone leave clothes between the cars? Were they on their way to the Salvation Army and dropped a pile? I kept cleaning towards the back of the car because I didn't really want to know what it was. When I got to the boots at the end of a pair of pants, I could fool myself no longer. There were sockless legs sticking out of those boots. There was a person in the snowdrift. My heart was thudding so loudly I was sure it would attract others.

"Hey there, you're out early." I staggered back as though the person in the snow had spoken. It was only my neighbour Steve coming up behind his car. My terrified look must have alerted him. "What's wrong?"

"I... I..." I could get no further. He rounded the end of the car and looked where I was looking.

"What the...? Is that a person? Who is it?" His expression mirrored my own. Together we gently removed the rest of the snow from the upper part of the body. Andy, looking very surprised, very dead, stared back at us. It was too late for help. He must have been dead for a long time. There was no snow under him. Around his head frozen blood shone like a halo.

7:10 a.m. We stepped back and I took my cell out of its zippered pocket. I keyed 911, gave the details and listened to the standard advice to not disturb the scene. No one mentioned the word 'murder' but there was a lot of blood for someone who had accidently fallen. What do I know? We would have to wait.

I don't know why, but I started to video the scene with my cell. "What are you doing?" Steve was outraged and tried to block me. "You can't take pictures."

"I'm not." I said, side-stepping him. "I'm making a video."

Okay, so I was splitting hairs. I wasn't about to stop and I didn't want interference. I walked slowly back and forth getting as close as my stomach would allow. I recorded the surrounding territory, walking only in those areas I had already shoveled. The fresh snow would not help. There would be no footprints to find the guilty party. If Andy was killed before the snow fell, it would cover any evidence below. So, why was I doing it? I assumed it was murder but why was I investigating?

It wasn't long before we heard the sirens. I quickly sent the video to my email. I knew Steve would tell the police what I did, and I was going to have to turn the cellphone over to them. That was okay by me as long as I had a copy.

Ken and Lisa were coming to see what was going on, with their little twins trotting behind them.

"Stop them, quick." I said, giving Steve something to do. He hurried in their direction before the kids could see the body. I could hear him talking in a harsh whisper as police and ambulance roared up the driveway.

7:20 a.m. All hell broke loose as people started to come out of their condos to see what the noise was about. The police officers took over and taped the area to keep the curious at bay. The crowd stayed at the edges trying to see over the cars and emergency workers in the weak morning light. I'm sure they were all wondering what Steve and I were doing there, and what was beside the car being examined. I saw Barb, Steve's wife, shivering with cold, not wanting to go inside while Steve couldn't.

We were interviewed then told to stay out. The police didn't seem too interested in my 'murder' theory. Most likely he fell in the dark and hit his head. Steve must have forgotten the video so I volunteered the information. As predicted, my cell phone was confiscated but I think they only took it to humour me. I was told I could get it back at the police station after they had reviewed the contents. Good thing I kept my landline.

7:40 a.m. A collective groan was heard as the body was covered and loaded into the ambulance. Finally, the crowd could see what it was but not who it was. I was sure some would find their way to my door or Steve's. The police gave us the standard warning to not speak to anyone and to make ourselves available when contacted.

I was finally able to move my car from beside the refuse bins to the visitors' lot so it was not blocking any more vehicles in the small parking lot. I walked back to my condo amid the stares of my neighbours. Only a few asked if I was okay. The majority just gawked. I didn't see where Steve went, although I was sure he wanted to be away from prying eyes as much as I did.

7:50 a.m. I watched a steady stream of people going past my windows so I knew the police were still in the parking lot. They would be there for as long as it took to collect what evidence existed and interview people to find out who knew what.

Andy was dead. I didn't know what to make of it. He was a nice young man in spite of his reputation. Some men called him 'randy Andy', a few women called him 'candy Andy'. To me, he was just 'handy Andy'.

8:00 a.m. I remembered the video. I couldn't think of why I had taken it in the first place. I wasn't sure I could look at it. But I did.

There was Andy lying cold and alone beside Steve's car. Had he fallen there or been attacked there? Had he crawled there after an attack? What would the autopsy reveal? I could see he had dressed in a hurry. His boots were not done up and he wore no socks. I thought irrationally that his legs would be so cold. Even his jacket was not done up... wait... the jacket?

Andy had the jacket of a young man, a navy Apex by Over the Edge. He was so proud of it. This jacket wasn't Andy's. It was navy but old-style and baggy. So, why was he wearing it and where had I seen it before?

It took me only seconds to remember; I saw it almost every day during the winter. On my way home from work I would meet Steve on his way to work wearing the jacket. What was Steve wearing this morning? The Apex! They were wearing each other's jackets. Both navy, both padded.

Now I knew why I made the video even though it didn't register at the time. The jacket triggered my subconscious.

Andy had been in Steve's house... with Barb... Steve came home early and found them together. Andy must have dressed in a hurry and grabbed the wrong jacket in the dark? Barb was shivering earlier not from cold but from fear. That was why Steve was in the parking lot and not at work. He knew Andy was there somewhere. His surprise was not from the discovery of the body but from my being there. He intended to change jackets before anyone else was up. And, I was the only one who knew it.

8:15 a.m. There was a banging at my door. I moved to the landline and dialed 911 for the second time that morning.

# Living My Dreams
## Silvia Alfaro

That trip from Austria to Switzerland in a clean, comfortable, fast train was so beautiful, so peaceful. I was a young woman, travelling alone, but I felt safe. There were two adolescents sitting in front of me, probably 17 or 18 years old. I didn't understand a word they said, as they were speaking in a foreign language, but I did notice that they looked happy and were joking with each other. They were tall, blond, very strong, had blue eyes and seemed like good kids.

They didn't make me feel unsafe. This is possibly because the men who had assaulted me in my home country looked entirely different. On two occasions, I was approached by a man with a knife, threatening to kill me if I didn't give him money or jewellery. On both occasions, the men were short, with dark hair and dark eyes. Neither looked strong, but both were armed. Fortunately, I was able to give both of them what they were asking for. I didn't suffer any physical injuries, but I was left emotionally hurt.

On the other hand, everything in Europe seemed so safe, so civilized, where women of all ages could travel alone without any problem. My hotel in Vienna was so beautiful that I felt like a queen sleeping in a room of a palace. The incredible thing was the price; it was much cheaper than student hostels in other European countries. Being young and not having a lot of money, a hotel like this one was a dream come true.

As a matter of fact, the whole trip was a dream come true. I was 24 and I had graduated from university two years before. I was finally an architect after years of arduous work; studying day and night, designing, drawing and building models. After graduation, I worked hard to save money for this trip.

I planned to spend one month exploring various European countries, visiting specific buildings and museums, followed by another month in Spain, where I planned to visit mainly universities. I had already collected information about Spanish universities' programs and key people I wanted to contact. Furthermore, I had brought my portfolio to show them. It contained the most important projects I had completed in university. I was looking forward to finding a program to continue my studies in architecture and pursue my dreams.

My family was middle class. We didn't have much money, but we lived in a big house full of art. We didn't have a car, but we were surrounded by books and paintings. We didn't have the newest colour television like the ones our friends had, but we had a beautiful piano and other musical instruments. We didn't go to restaurants, but our table was always an amazing symphony of delicious dishes made with love by my mother. The atmosphere in our home was harmonious and pleasant.

But when we opened the front door of our house, the contrast was shocking. We lived in a central area of the city, which was very busy and had many pedestrians and cars. It seemed that everything you might see in a city was within a few blocks. If we walked to the east we'd be in a beautiful neighbourhood with gorgeous houses backed by beautifully forested mountains, while if we walked just one block to the west we'd be on noisy, busy, chaotic streets with old buses and cars constantly sounding their horns and spewing black clouds of exhaust.

There were also homeless people everywhere. Sometimes, in the nearby shopping area, we would see people with deformities, or without arms or without legs, sitting on the sidewalks asking for money. It rained a lot there, and I remember how I loved to hear the rain when I was in bed, cozy under the blankets. But at the same time, I remember wondering how I could enjoy it, knowing that at that very moment there were hundreds of kids on the streets, taking refuge under bridges or in smelly, rat-infested sewers. So, I fell asleep with feelings of sadness and guilt.

Ever since I was very young, I dreamed of travelling around the world. My parents grew up reading the classics and listening to European music, so they had extensive knowledge of literature, visual arts, music, history and much more. Most of the things I knew were learned through the conversations that took place in our household and through reading the books my parents had.

Silvia Alfaro

That's why the trip to Europe was so special to me. I was finally able to visit those marvellous cities I had only seen through books. Now, I was walking on those streets, where I didn't see people who made me uncomfortable, and where I enjoyed being able to have my camera out at all times without the fear of being robbed. I admired the cathedrals, the museums and the palaces. All the gardens were so beautiful, with a perfect landscape design. For me, everything was fascinating.

On that train trip, everything looked perfect from my window. I was only in the first of the eight weeks I had planned to stay in Europe, but I already had the idea of coming back to study for many years, and possibly staying permanently if I could finish a Masters Degree and find a job as an architect. I was seriously considering moving to Europe if I could, as I felt a level of safety I had never experienced in my home country.

I was travelling fairly light. I had my passport, air tickets, travellers' cheques and cash in my security belt, and I had a camera hanging from my neck at all times. But most importantly, I had my backpack, which contained everything I needed in order to make my dreams a reality. I have to admit that it was actually a big one; it contained not only my clothes and a few books, but also my architecture portfolio and many rolls of film. My plan was to document as many buildings as I could—particularly the ones on the list I'd made—so that at the end of the two months I would have an amazing collection of photographs, which I would eventually use to teach the history of architecture. I had my future in that backpack.

I clearly remember dreaming about my future in Europe during that train trip. I had a lot of time to do that, as it was approximately an eight-hour trip. Suddenly, I felt hungry and decided to treat myself to a nice meal. When I got to the dining car, I was surprised to see how elegant it was, with tablecloths and all the other details needed for an extraordinary experience. It was particularly special to me since I had never seen luxury on a train. The only other times I had travelled by train was when I was very young on a train called *El Expreso del Sol*. My family would take the 18-hour train trip from my home city to a town in the coast where my maternal grandparents lived. At the time, travelling by train was much cheaper than travelling by airplane.

So, for a big family who didn't have a car, the train was the better option. However, this one was uncomfortable and noisy. It rocked so much that it was impossible to have a cup of coffee without spilling half of it. The bathrooms were dirty and smelly. Honestly, the service was terrible. I don't remember there being a dining car on that train, so when I saw this one in Europe I was delighted and decided to eat well and enjoy myself. While I was savouring my delicious meal the train stopped at Innsbruck. I admired all the movement on the platform: people coming in and going out, families with happy kids, and young travellers like me.

When the train departed from that station, I felt a sharp pain in my heart and my stomach. Fear overcame me. I rushed back to my car and when I arrived I saw my leather jacket on my seat. The two young men were not there, and my backpack—along with my dreams—was gone.

# A Mother's Choice
## Jessica Clarke

"Please, please, please, please..." I beg hoarsely.

I burrow my forehead deeper into his neck, against his rapidly cooling skin. The sobs wracking my body have subsided to pitiful whimpers. There's no telling how long I've been crouched here, my glassy eyes sightless to the small crowd gathered to gawk, their voracious appetites for tragedy drawing their attention, but not one offered their assistance as I screamed for help until my voice was hoarse. Not one.

The pressure of a gentle hand on my shoulder snaps me back to my surroundings. I blink tears from my lashes as my eyes cut to my left, seeking the owner of the hand. Confused, I glance at the people standing nearby, surrounding us, but notice no one standing near enough to touch me. I can't tell if I'm seeing things, but everyone seems to be still.

Unmoving. Impossible.

Could this be why no one answered my cries for help?

Somehow while the world around us seems to have gone still, I am able to move. The disparity of emotions gathered on their faces reminds me of the masks actors in Japanese comical theater wear; their faces twisted into exaggerated interpretations of horror, fright and glowers. These masks make up the frozen tableau decorating my grief, looking on as I shatter in pieces before them. As the only thing good I'd ever done with my life dies.

I shiver at the cool draft of air whispering against my neck and glance back down to my sons' ashen face just in time to watch his overlong bangs flutter in the same breeze. He'd been due to have his hair cut for weeks now, but somehow, he'd convinced me to grow it out.

I shift his weight in my arms and reach a bloody, trembling hand to his face. I move the mass of dark waves off his brow and drag a gentle finger across his cheek, smearing a bright crimson streak across his pale skin. Another hiccupped sob escapes my lips as I pull him into me, rocking his limp body in time with mine.

I'm alone now.

My angel's gone. He has left me, taking my heart with him.

I inhale deeply, noting the fragrant traces of our laundry and his shampoo in the air. It feels as though the smells are already disappearing, floating away on the breeze. Leaving me too.

His beautiful green eyes? Closed? Evermore. They will never again look up at me with the wondrous joys of childhood. His parted lips will never draw breath again. He'll never smile at me in impish exuberance or tell me he loves me... They will forever remain still.

My heart bleeds in agony at the precious miracle I've lost.

My baby.

My son.

A strangled cry passes my lips as I crush his little body to my chest.

How can anything ever matter again?

Pitiful sounds continue to claw their way up my throat, sounding more strangled by the second. I can't breathe.

"He's gone home now."

A tiny, pale hand lands on my son's head, drawing my unfocused gaze. Crouched before us is a little girl, not a day older than my son. Her appearance is nondescript. She looks just like any other doled out six-year-old girl, with her curly pigtails and yellow floral summer dress. She's even holding a purple lollipop in her other hand. But her eyes; there's something odd about her eyes. Looking into them you glimpse the stars and constellations, a vastness beyond her tender years. They are ageless.

"W-who are you?"

She gives me a sad, enigmatic smile as she straightens from her knees to stand back closer to the ever still crowd.

"No, wait! Please don't go!" I beg of her. "Please help me save him."

She frowns at me as though puzzled I'd ask such a thing.

"He cannot be saved. I brought him home," she replies.

"What?"

Faced with my dumbfounded expression she elaborates. "I brought his soul home. Once a soul crosses over, there is no going back. Nothing in this world could save him. It's too late now, I'm sorry."

Another sob rips from me. Crossed over? Too late? I drag my eyes away from her sad face and look down at my world. The harder I try to focus, to memorize his features, the harder my vision blurs. The rivulets of tears streaming down my face in wide, unruly tracks, slide down to my neck and pool in my sons' hair.

It can't be too late.

"He can't be gone. He just can't." I ignore the pity lining her childlike features. "If you really are some kind of angel, then bring him back," I whisper to the girl over his head. My voice is barely audible, hoarse from the rawness of too many tears, but I know she heard me.

The grim twist of her lips tells me she's not indifferent to my pleas.

"I cannot help you. I do not deliver souls; I collect them."

A collector of souls... as if my son's life is akin to a grim reaper's stamp. Like a lone spark to kindling that's been left out in the sun to dry for too long. Fury ignites in my chest. Its savage heat licks like flames across my body and eventually settles in the barren crevice where my heart used to be.

"Bring him back!"

I want to rage at her stoic calm in the face of my agony. How could anyone with a heart rip a child away from his mother? I want to beat my fists and wage war with all the wrath of a grieving mother against whoever made the rules.

"He'll never come back, will he?" I ask, defeat clouding my voice.

"No."

That one word has the power to rip me to shreds anew. My skin burns. I can't contain all the grief and rage boiling beneath its surface.

Lashing out, I snap, "So then why are you just standing there? To watch me suffer?"

"I am still here because I am not done."

Her vague statement says nothing at all, but it does revive my dwindling hope. I can still save my boy. As though struck by a bolt of lightning I stop yelling and gently lay my son's prone body to the ground before rising to my feet. Arms stretched wide, I look down into her infinite eyes and plead, "Take me instead!

Bring him back and I'll gladly give my life for his."

She's already shaking her head at me, her curly pigtails swaying long before I finish.

"I don't understand!" I shout. I do a slow spin, ready to beg the first passerby to help, but they are all frozen. The couple holding hands next to me stares down in horror where my son's body lies, lifeless. A distracted man clutching a cellphone to his ear appears startled as if he was just jolted out of whatever place he was a moment ago. Across the street, a young man no older than 20 is frozen in midstride. His long legs would allow him to eat up the distance in an instant if he were still running.

To my right there's a small group of high school students carrying backpacks on their shoulders who are obviously cutting class this afternoon, all gripping each other close, fear etched on their faces. And finally, my eyes settle on the banner for the doctor's office across the intersection and just two doors down. Where my son was going to get a check-up today.

Less than 70 feet and we would've walked into the office to be blasted by a gust of air conditioning. Less than 70 feet to safety. The distance between affectionate exasperation and bone-crushing despair. The chasm between life and death.

Seventy feet.

"To collect."

I'm wrenched out of my anguished musings and back to the little girl who somehow must've stopped time, freezing all of the people rushing to and fro on this busy street. Maybe she was really here to prolong my pain. To draw this moment out, to make me suffer beyond what I already can't endure.

As if reading my mind the girl adds, "You."

I go still. My mind races 1,000 miles a second as I struggle to make sense of what she's saying. Then, like a second bolt of lightning striking me in as many minutes, my muscles go lax and I crumple to my knees.

With effort, I manage to spread myself over my son's body and rest my head over his quiet chest.

My relief is indescribable; beyond profound. In an instant, all the grief that had been ravaging my insides is extinguished, and it's replaced by joy. Pure, unfiltered joy; and love. As long as I have my son, anything else is trivial.

Besides, I'd leave nothing and no one behind. There is nothing on this earth tethering me to it, but him.

"Will I be with him?"

I lift my head to watch as she tilts hers up, her unfathomable gaze going sightless for what appears to be an eternity. My breath gushes out sharply when she gives me a cheerful smile. Feeling as if I've just run a marathon, I look down at my son one last time. Raising my hands to cup his cheeks I lay a kiss on his brow and whisper, "It's alright baby, mommy's coming home too."

I let him go, to stand, doubt never crossing my mind. If anyone had asked me before this exact moment what choice I would make in this instant, my decision would've been the same. It's really no choice at all.

With one last glance at the collector, I step back into the oncoming traffic and wait for time to resume.

# A Nice Cup of Tea
## Keith Newton

Clutching the letter, Alex shuffled back along the dingy hallway and mounted the creaky stairs to his bare, bleak room. Badly lit by a single unshaded bulb dangling from the crusty ceiling, his cell, as he thought of it, offered scant comfort. A makeshift bed held an untidy tangle of blankets and clothes. The other furniture consisted of a plastic chair and a rickety table, at which he now sat.

Morosely he contemplated the walls of the drafty little space. Dozens of slips of paper of varying sizes and colours, pasted, taped, some pinned, all bore the same message: rejection. A cup of tea! That was it. Might help; can't hurt. He placed the battered kettle on the temperamental burner.

Sipping the tea he plucked up courage and with trembling fingers opened the envelope with the publisher's logo on the top-left corner. Of course, he knew it. Yet another one. Number 82.

He thought back to his momentous decision of a few months ago. His parents had tried to dissuade him. *Don't be silly, young man. We want you to take over the business, of course. Family name. Think what you're giving up!*

But he was determined. His head spun with the idea of expressing himself, his true self, in a way that would set him alongside the greats. The greats, few of whom he had actually read; none completely.

*But the castle, the yacht, your Lamborghini, the polo ponies. Think again. The writer's life is not so glamorous. You'll probably end up destitute in a garret.*

Mama and Papa had cajoled, begged. He was steadfast. The inevitable storm brewed and burst with a screaming rant from his father that ended with the scion's immediate expulsion from the mansion. Disowned, banished.

At first, as he stood by the bus stop with his hastily-retrieved wallet and a backpack full of clothes and notebooks, dictionary and pens, he thought this was cool, neat. Exciting even: the bus ride from the village near his ancestral home was an exhilarating and totally new experience. He was enthusiastic, brimming with ideas, supremely self-confident. He couldn't wait to take up the draft of his story once again, polish it to a high sheen, and send it off to a lucky publisher.

The early days of his Spartan existence had been rather a lark. After all, it wouldn't be long before fame and fortune came along. In fact, the waiting became nerve-wracking. Then came the first rejection. At first he was incredulous. There must be some mistake. Slowly it dawned on him that of course not all publishers were so discerning as to recognize the excellence of his truly extraordinary story. He'd try one of the big houses. No, wait, maybe several. Just in case there existed some other benighted editor who might not recognize his brilliance. But if, as he was sure, many publishers would soon be clamouring for his work, he could play them off to secure the best possible deal.

But the weeks dragged agonizingly by without the expected triumph. Around the ninth week the seeds of doubt began to take root. He steeled himself, considered his dwindling resources, and signed up for a writer's workshop.

Alex was shaken. He was chastened by the new-found knowledge that a short story might usefully embody certain features such as a plot, place, timeframe, action, a character or two, and a central issue, along with dimensions such as mystery, tension, emotion. His faith in his own unique, radical, unstructured, unfiltered, stream-of-consciousness, highly personal style was rudely rattled. Maybe he should try to write in what he had so far haughtily dismissed as a brutally formulaic style; 'method writing' he called it. Just for a while; just long enough to satisfy the Philistines and get my foot in the door, he decided. Then I can show the world some real writing. But disappointment became disillusionment and eventually despair.

He sipped again. Reflected. Some faint glimmers of hope tried bravely but unsuccessfully to pierce his pall of gloom. Manfully he contemplated reality. Reality, he was forced to admit, was really not much fun. Shreds of disbelief still hung on: how could those idiot publishers fail to recognize greatness? Even after he had lowered himself to the straitjacket of what the workshop leader had called the "default third person." Hiding his brilliant personal, individual light under a bushel! Even after actually *thinking* about a story before writing. Plot, characters, all that sadly outdated, reactionary, irrelevant, structured... he grimaced... stuff.

Another sip. The tea was ghastly. A far cry from the rich black Oolong blends of Assam and Ceylon and the champagne of teas from Darjeeling. More like the sweepings from some dreadful warehouse floor. Ah, yes, reality. He missed the car, the polo, the use of the jet, the marinas on exotic isles. *God, it's cold in here.*

Seventeen seconds and his mind was made up. He shuffled to the door, down the stairs, along the passage to the gloomy vestibule with its long-suffering payphone and the tattered directory hanging dejectedly on its chain. He pulled out a pocketful of change. He knew the number by heart. Dialed confidently. Waited.

He could picture the scene at the other end of the line: the chateau in the French Alps, the salon with the ancestral portraits, the Astrakhan rugs, sparkling crystal. He pictured the tall elegant dowager: immaculate steel-grey coiffure, slender manicured fingers around the slim stem of the day's first Martini, a mildly inquisitive look on the patrician face as she lifted the solid gold receiver.

"Hello, Nana. It's Alexander. May I come and stay a while?"

# About Poetry
## Majid Kafai

Poetry is powerful beautiful words
    composed in a sensational way
Poetry is a noble play in which The Lords of Creativity
With harmonious words masterfully play.

Poetry is an artistic display, a golden tray on which
The diamonds of intellect are carried away.

Poetry is the crown of prose, a perfumed rose
Inside which our sentiments repose.

Poetry is the dance of words
    inside the ballroom of reflection
Poetry is about communication and connection.

Poetry is inspiration
A nice painting from the gallery of imagination.

Poetry is imagery
The source of imagery, is creativity
The source of creativity, is talent
Poetry is talent in action.

Poetry is friend of peace and construction
Enemy of war and destruction.

Poetry has the character of spring showers
It comes suddenly with fresh flowers.

Poetry is a heavenly light
It is the juice of insight
The harvest of the bright
A flight to the land of dream and delight.

Poetry is
The fire of love
The flame of adoration
The pain of separation
The union elation.
Poetry is the stream of desires
The blaze of jealousy fires
The eruption of feelings

A sort of deliverance
Self–healing.

Poetry is the window of liberty
Inside the prison of loneliness
Poetry is the wine of happiness.

Poetry is self-examination
Revelation and relaxation combined.

Poetry is love of homeland
And carrying in exile
The heavy luggage of humiliation
With a broken hand.

Poetry is sensitivity
Is seeing the invisible tears of a caged bird
Always dreaming to be as free as the white clouds
Constantly wishing to run away from its jailer
The sinner Mankind.

Poetry is the rain of blessing
    over the thirsty desert of sorrow
Poetry is a shelter, it is also the poet's arrow.

Poetry is the melody of heart
The perfume of soul
The mirror of mind
Poetry to injustice is not blind.

Poetry is the wisdom torch
Illuminating life's dark porch.

Poetry is the pain of a free thinker
A poison drinker
Enchained in the prison of tyranny
His sin believing in democracy and justice
Kindness and tolerance.

Poetry is the loudspeaker of freedom
The voice of the voiceless
A costly social dress.

Poetry is about wondering
Who? The Creator is
And how? From nothing
He created the whole world!
Marveling from where? We all came

And to where? We all go
One by one, in a row.

Poetry is understanding
The sanctity of life
Preserving the beauty of nature
Respecting the purity of water and air
Poetry is about care.

Poetry is seeing one's picture
In the frame of death
Poetry is appreciating
The value of each breath.

Poetry is thanking
The Lord for giving us life
Poetry is hard work, a mental strife.

Finally
What is good poetry
Bad poetry and
Pure poetry?

*Beauty*
Is the essence of good poetry
Which silently yet powerfully
Touches our heart.

Good poetry is a jewel
A precious piece of art
Bad poetry is none of these
It is just a pebble
Carried on a squeaky cart!

And what is pure poetry?
It is a fascinating rainbow
Over the gate of times
It is the gong of beauty
Which in the tower of humanity
Forever chimes…

# Oh Brother
## Keith Newton

*F*ree! At least for the rest of the day. Meg had survived another tough lunchtime shift in the rowdy bar of the village's lone hotel. Now she would drive into town, shop a bit then meet Jeff for dinner. Undaunted by the leaden sky, she cheerfully guided her small sensible car out onto the riverside road to the city...

Dazed, trembling a little, she checked again. Nothing broken. Just an allover pain that promised a lot of bruises, and a gash on the forehead. Thank heaven for seatbelts. She stared bleakly at the sad, crumpled wreck. Sighed. Black ice, she guessed ruefully. Certainly she'd had no warning of the sudden slide that resulted from the merest touch on the brake as she'd entered the bend.

Silence, cold stillness and a menacing dark sky. The wind picked up. It began to snow. She shuffled to the edge of the deserted road, winced and wiped the blood from her forehead. Cursed. Prayed.

A dark shape loomed through the blowing snow. A van approached, slid, corrected, slid again and stopped. A window lowered and a voice yelled, "Hey! Get in."

Clutching her bag she clambered inside. Two men. Menacing. Vaguely familiar.

"What happened?" asked the passenger.

"Skidded", she explained. "Slammed into the rail. Car's a wreck. Totaled."

"You okay? You're bleeding."

"Shook up. Everything hurts. Bump on the head."

Judging by the stream of profanity, the driver was having difficulty with the road conditions. She was now also aware of the unmistakable aroma of booze. Her furtive glances confirmed her suspicion. Her rescuers were the two uncouth regulars at the pub where she worked.

"I know you! Hey, Brad, look what we got here. It's the girl from the Shamrock. You know, the looker... with the body."

He pulled back the hood of her parka, took off her woolen hat, grinned lasciviously, triumphantly.

"Yeah, that's better. Our lucky day, Brad."
She prayed fervently.
Brad was in no mood for jollity: "Gotta get rid of this fuckin' van. I told you we shouldn't have taken it. Shouldn't have stopped for her either. Goddam cops'll be lookin' for us already."
"No sweat, Brad. Soon as we get into town we dump it. Then disappear. We all go for a friendly drink." He turned to Meg, "How's that sound, darlin'? We'll take good care of you. Here, sweetie, take some of this."
His hand tightened on her knee as he thrust the bottle toward her face. She prayed harder.
Approaching the city, as they slowed for a light, a police cruiser pulled neatly in ahead of them and stopped with lights flashing. Two officers emerged and came to the van.
"May I see your license and ownership, sir?"
The other officer appeared at the passenger door. Relief. Joy. She burst out of the van and leapt into the arms of the beaming policeman.
"Jeff! I... I w-was just coming to see you," she stammered.
"I know, Sis, I know."

# Message to Aylan
## Qais Ghanem

I know that millions have shed their tears
And others expressed their morbid fears
That the powers that be, do not really care
About those who starve, or those who run
About those who die by the sword or the gun
Whose flesh is shredded by the stealthy drones
When wedding songs turn suddenly to groans
Then the wedding cake is served at the wake
While they just repeat: it was just a mistake!
And the rich and mighty, their shock they fake

Was it ever a mistake that you should drown?
When you, your brother, your mum and dad
Had to run for your lives and leave your town
And part with all for dinghy space
To escape to Canada, or other place
In search of a home with a strong roof above
To rest your heavy head, surrounded by love
To wake up next day to laugh and play
And fight with Ghalib like brothers do
And paint with crayons, red, green and blue.

But it was no mistake, my little innocent friend!
When life is at stake, are we not supposed to bend
Those rules of immigration, and shelve that book
With eyes and heart, of compassion to look
At the plight of *Reihana* and her little boys
Deprived of shelter, water, and toys
Wherever they come from, whichever be their town
Whatever their colour, black, white or brown

But millions of tears were shed in your name
When the world saw your tiny floating frame

And the name of *Aylan*, will never be the same
Face down in the water, with your lungs full of salt
Your little nostrils plugged up with sand
Because people in this world, both here and around
Where farms and rivers and lakes surround
Where tons of food in garbage bins are found
Where water and nectar and wine abound
Did not want your kind to share their land!

# The Soul Eggs
## Laurie Stewart

"I can't go on, we'll die out here."

The man turned in time to see his wife stumble, dropping the small child she carried into a snow bank. The wind howled laughter as it picked up, blowing stinging shards of frozen snow against their cheeks.

He walked back, numbed feet shifting on the snow covered path, and tenderly picked the boy up, checking him for injury. He was alive, his cheeks white with frostbite.

The man nodded. "Take the boy home. It's too cold for him."

As she took the small body from her husband, the woman asked quietly, "What will you do out here alone? Holy Sunday is nearly over."

"I can't give up, she was my mother."

"Come home to me. Don't die before me, I couldn't survive."

The man shrugged; he had no choice but to go on. If he didn't find it by midnight, at least he could comfort himself with the knowledge that he had tried.

The path was nearly invisible in the dark, a barely seen ribbon against the deeper snow. The moon grazed the tops of the trees on the other side of the river, the stars stared, unblinking, in the clarity of the night. He could tell by the hard, unmoving shadows his torch made, the way his breath hung in the air as if solid... it was almost midnight.

There had been no sign of the Egg. He only had one Egg this year, but he knew exactly what to look for; they shimmered like starlight, like the sun on the rippling shallows of the rock pool by the river. He had always found them, but this year the beast might win. And he could fail. Fail in his last duty.

The man paused, watching the icy wind make shapes from the flying snow, and considered. He had checked all of the usual hiding spots in the daylight. Under the hedgerows, in the barn and chicken coop, even in the house.

This year was different, the beast wanted him to fail, and he knew it. It was the second week of April, a month past the Equinox. The weather should be much warmer, the snow gone. This unseasonable weather, so like the depths of February, meant the beast was cheating. How do you find an Egg in snow so deep?

At least he was dressed for the weather, hand knit wool socks and leggings under his leather wraps. He wore not one wool vest, but two. Plus a heavy fur lined cloak. And still he froze. The wind found gaps in his clothing and streaked fingers of ice across his skin. His nose was numb, its dripping frozen to his beard.

The man stumbled, falling to his knees. His feet were past numb, frozen, unfeeling. His hands burned whenever he touched the snow. He closed his eyes to rest for a moment, then struggled to open them when the wind tried to freeze them shut. His thoughts circled around and around. He had to find the Egg by midnight.

In the silence of the night, a sound beckoned him, the swift burbling of the water over rocks at the river's edge. It called him, a bright promise of silver water, quick in the moonlight. No, the beast would not be so cruel. But it fit, the Egg would shimmer like ice glazed water, sparkle like dancing shoals at the shore.

He found the river's edge by stumbling through the thin ice. Water soaked through his boots in an instant. The leather he had wrapped around his calves to keep out the snow and wind did nothing to keep out the frigid water. His breath hitched in shock as icy fire lanced his feet and lower legs. He staggered forward, fumbling for traction on unfelt rocks.

The beast was already crowing its victory. He could hear the ragged howl from the woods, it rose, deafening, then faded away. The night was silent, save for the icy singing of the water.

Then he saw it. Subtly glowing through the rippled water where the currents from the river spun into the rock pool. It was in deep water, already the ice crusts bumped his legs above his boots, and the Egg was further in. He lurched forward on legs that had been frozen into dead stumps. His face burned where drops of water sprayed him, as if sprayed with acid. It was his mother. If he failed, she was truly cursed.

The water seemed to hiss in triumph as it swirled up his thighs to his waist. He slipped on a mossy stone, his flailing arms spraying more searing, icy droplets on his face. He was close now. The Egg sat at the bottom of the pool. He would need to immerse himself completely to reach it.

He stared at the water, seeing in full the trick the beast has played. To save his mother's soul, he would need to die. There would be no surviving a full soaking, followed by walking home through the bitter cold.

He closed his eyes, offering up a prayer for his own soul. If he died tonight, he would serve the beast for a full year, until Holy Sunday came around again. But it would be worth it, to save his mother's soul from an eternity in the beast's service.

As a child, he had loved to search for the Eggs, delighted by their beauty and the clever places they were hidden. His mother had shielded him from the truth. It was no game. Anyone who died in winter, who could not be buried quickly on sacred ground, ended up in service to the beast. There was only this day, this one chance to save their souls. He had from dawn to midnight, or the beast would win.

Sloshing heavily, he moved as close to the Egg as he could without risking stepping on it. He took a deep breath and ducked underwater. Burning pain flared across all of his skin. His breath threatened to explode from his lungs.

Swirling silt obscured his vision. He felt for the egg with deadened fingers. A seductive voice told him to give up.

But he thought of his son, growing up without a father. Life in the valley would be impossible for a widow with children. He kept searching.

Unless his thrashing had made it roll away. Stars flashed a beckoning welcome behind his eyelids. Reassuring warmth crept up his lifeless limbs... He was dying.

He sensed more than felt, the Egg. Beneath his hand. Carefully, he used both hands to scoop it up, to clutch it to his chest, as he fought to stand. The water grabbed at him, reluctant to give up its prize.

But finally he stood. The Egg was found, his mother was saved. He turned toward the bank, faintly surprised by the thin sheet of ice that cracked and fell from his clothing as he shifted.

The water froze his hair and beard into icicles, his eyes froze shut when he blinked.
He smiled. Warmth embraced him. Deep inside, he knew that this was a bad sign, but he was so tired. He couldn't raise the energy to move. Vaguely, he wondered if they would find him in the morning, still standing, his Egg clutched to his chest.
He thought he heard his wife's voice, and was glad that she would be the last thing he thought of.

The woman stood on the bank, bundled in many layers against the cold. Watching as her brother leapt into the half-frozen rock pool to pull her husband out of the water. She winced at his gasp, and stifled curses as his legs and feet went instantly numb at the touch of the icy water.
She prayed through clenched teeth, a heartfelt plea to the darkness to let her husband return to her. Terrified that they were too late.
The two men stumbled to the bank, her husband falling, unmoving into the snow, to lay on his back, barely breathing.
"I found it." His voice was weak, almost hidden by the sudden howling of wind and beasts in the forest.
The woman snapped into movement, pulling a blanket from her shoulders to bundle her husband.
"We must get him moving, he'll die if we don't get him home."
Her brother nodded, and pulled the man to his feet. Boneless, he folded over, and was lifted onto the brother's shoulders. His wife wrapped the rough wool blanket around him. His hands hung down, past the end of his brother-in-law's coat, still clutching the Egg. His hands were white and unmoving.

They reached the house and slipped into the warmth and light of the fire. Stiff and barely seeming to breathe, her husband was settled on a blanket on the hearth. The wife went to fetch water for tea, and to gently warm his frozen skin.
"I found it." He whispered.
"You're a fool," his wife's brother replied. "That damned beast has it in for you, and you just walk out into the river in a storm? What if you had died? What would my sister do?"

"She was my mother not yours. I don't expect you to understand."

"I understand all right. I understand that you put your guilt over your mother's death ahead of my nephew's survival. Did you think of him? Did you think what it would be like to have a father in the beast's service? The pressure on him to save you?"

"Enough. He's home, and safe now." His wife walked softly across the floor, a bowl of barely warmed water held out. She crouched by her husband, sliding his frozen hands into the water. She ignored his hiss of pain as she pried the Egg out of his grasp.

It has faded, dulled. It no longer shines and shimmers; it is a flat dark blue, or maybe brown. The light has gone from within it. She placed it carefully in a basket on the mantel. A basket with two other Eggs, also faded and dull. The Eggs her brother found for his wife's family would stay here, safe.

"We found them all this year. Come the hottest day of summer, we'll break them to let the souls go free; maybe the beast will be satisfied."

The man nodded as violent shivering overtook him. He knew the beast would never be satisfied. That's why the beast cheated. When the man was a boy, you had three days to find your eggs, from Good Friday to Easter Monday. But now there was only Holy Sunday, dawn until midnight. After that, the rabbit won, and any souls still imprisoned in the Eggs were lost for eternity.

# A Little Harmless Flirtation
## Maggie Taylor

"Jenny, please. You have to stop." Dunstan placed a restraining hand over hers as she grabbed the handle.

"Oh Dunstan, don't be so dull." With her free hand Jenny pried his fingers loose and turned to face him.

"You promised," he whined. "We've had to move three times in the past two years."

Jenny measured his mood, trying to decide the quickest way out of the door. Mollify or exasperate. It would take too long to calm her husband; besides the alternative was such fun. "Dear, dear Dunstan, the only reason I agreed to sell our lovely Rockcliffe home and move into a retirement residence was for the recreation. I need excitement. I need the stimulus of meeting new people, trying new things."

"Our home was not in Rockcliffe. It was in Manor Park."

"Close enough."

"And what you're doing is upsetting people."

Jenny took a few steps back into the living room. "If people are upset it's because they lack a sense of humour. I'm just having a little fun."

"It's only fun if others are laughing, and I assure you most of them haven't been. Twice now management has suggested we might be happier at another facility; one more suited to your…" Dunstan's lip began twitching, "*exceptionally gregarious disposition.*"

"There, see? They recognized my need for a more invigorating environment, and they were unselfish enough to say so."

Dunstan was dumbfounded. "Just how were they unselfish?"

Jenny allowed just a hint of irritation to leak. "Because they put my needs before the megabucks they'd milk from us if we stayed."

"You just don't get it do you? '*Exceptionally gregarious disposition*' was a euphemism for '*we want you to move because you are a royal pain in the ass*'."

"Uh, uh, uh. Don't be vulgar Dunstan. You know I can't

abide vulgarity."

Defeated, Dunstan flopped into the enveloping comfort of his recliner. With him out of the way Jenny again seized the handle, and as the door shushed behind her she tossed a parting shot. "It's only a little harmless flirtation."

As Dunstan sank further back into the soft brown leather he closed his eyes and pictured Jenny making her way down to the piano lounge. She would pause at the gilt framed mirror and fuss with her hair, puffing it a few extra inches until it stood almost on end, then tug at her slinky blouse, exposing even more of her ample breasts. Although he was proud that his beautiful wife still retained her voluptuous curves—damn-it-all—but her curves were for his enjoyment and there she was flaunting them like some... like some... His eyes popped open. "Calm yourself," he said. He felt his heart beat slowing and as his breathing deepened he shut his eyes.

The elevator would stop at their floor and after a quick survey, Jenny would position herself to advantage ensuring that any man received full benefits. Dunstan felt a wave of heat rising and again chided himself. When surrounded by women, Jenny strove to make them jealous of her full figure. Through a gesture as innocent as smoothing her skirt, she would allow her hand a brief pause on the fullest curve while she focused on the other woman's bony hips. The ensuing eye contact between the women said it all. Dunstan remembered yesterday seeing the intense flash of anger in one woman's eyes as Jenny made her point. The glare this woman turned on Dunstan made him wither, wither all the way down. It was so humiliating. His left eyelid began twitching.

"Breathe deeply, man. Breathe. Inhale... exhale... in..."

Dunstan's arms flung outwards in the startle gesture of a newborn. With his heart rate and breathing gone all to hell he tried to understand what just happened. The damn phone. Another one of Jenny's experimental ring tones. It shrilled twice more before he was able to grab the receiver and punch 'talk'.

"Who is it?" he barked.

"Well, that's a fine way to answer the phone."

"Oh. Emmeline. Sorry."

"What's the matter?"

"I was doing some deep breathing exercises then this damn thing…"

"Another anxiety attack?"

"Not so bad. I almost have it under control."

"Let me guess. Jenny?"

"Who else? Oh, Emmeline," he moaned, "will it never end?"

"Only if you are willing to finally do something about it."

"I'm trying, I really am, but there's no reasoning with her. She doesn't seem to care that her flirting upsets others. I watch the women's faces as Jenny flounces about. They truly despise her. Nelly cornered me in the elevator and…"

"Who's Nelly?"

"Mrs Warner, wife of Tim. They live on the floor below us. She waited until Jenny left the elevator then grabbed my arm. She said, and I quote, 'It is bad enough that Jenny gets all kittenish with the single gentlemen when there are so few left for the other women, but Dunstan, really! She is nothing but a shameless hussy with other people's husbands.' I was taken aback."

"And so you should be."

"It gets worse. She said, 'If I ever catch Jenny offering her wares again to Tim, I will personally burn an A on her forehead with a live cigarette', and she dug her nails into my arm for emphasis."

"A for Adulteress? How quaint. And it would serve her right."

"Emmeline, you can't mean that."

"Oh, but I do. You know that I love you, and Jenny has absolutely no right to treat you that way," she ended with a huff.

"I shouldn't be talking to you about this."

"Well why not? We're friends and friends share."

"It's not right. What goes on between husband and wife should stay between husband and wife."

"You can be so old fashioned, Dunstan."

"Besides, Jenny would be really upset if she knew I was talking to you about our problems like this."

"She still resents our friendship, after all this time?"

"That hasn't changed, and it won't as long as you go on professing your undying love for me in front of her."

"Well, we do have a history, you and I. Come back to me

Dunstan. I can make your life peaceful and serene again."

"Goodbye, Emmeline."

"Don't hang up…"

But Dunstan couldn't disconnect fast enough. What was it with women? He slumped back into his chair then lunged at the phone and turned off the ringer. He tried some more relaxation techniques but drifted into a troubled sleep instead. He awoke an hour later, sweaty and disoriented.

"Jenny, are you here? No? No of course you're not home where you belong. What did you expect, Dunstan? Oh damn. Now I'm talking out loud to myself. That's not good, not good at all."

He staggered into the washroom and yanked open the medicine cabinet. What he needed was a good night's rest. A couple of sleeping pills should do it. No, the way he was feeling, three would be better. He tossed the empty bottle. Then his eyes focused on the bottle of Miltown. He couldn't remember if he'd taken his antianxiety meds today so he popped the last of those as well.

He stuck his head under the faucet, rubbed the back of his neck, rinsed his mouth, toweled his head half-heartedly, donned pajamas and flopped into the bed.

Hours later something disturbed his pleasant floating sensations.

"Mr Truman. It's the concierge. You didn't answer your phone sir."

In the interval between knockings, Dunstan drifted back into oblivion, only to be roused again.

"Sir, I have the police here." Heavier knocking was followed by, "Mr Truman, I have the key and I'm coming in."

Two officers entered Dunstan's apartment, closing the door on the concierge. They found Dunstan face down across the bed.

"Mr Truman, wake up sir… Dunstan Truman, you need to wake up." The detective turned to his partner, "Check around, see if you can find any drugs. This guy's really out of it."

"I found these empty bottles; prescriptions for Miltown and sleeping pills. Do you think he took an overdose?"

"Better request an ambulance. Help me turn him over first. Oh crap. That looks like blood on his shirt." The detective quickly checked Dunstan for injuries but found none. "Look around for more blood."

His partner called out from the bathroom, "There's some on a towel and nightgown hanging on the door… and some on a razor."

"Bag those for evidence. The blood could be from a shaving accident, or we're dealing with a murder-suicide. Call it in."

Dunstan regained consciousness in a hospital bed. His throat was raw. The doctor held a restraining hand on his shoulder. "Just lie back and relax sir. We had to pump your stomach."

Dunstan croaked, "What'd you do that for? I was just trying to get some sleep." He started coughing.

"Mr Truman. I am Detective Thorn and this is Constable Bastion…" Thorn moved into Dunstan's field of vision. "Sir, we need to ask you some questions. Is your wife's name Jenny?"

Dunstan nodded. "Can you tell me when you last saw your wife?"

Panic rose. "Jenny? Where's Jenny?"

"Can you tell me when you last saw her?"

Dunstan navigated his way through a muddle of floating images. "It was around eight… when that *chippy* went to strut her stuff," he sputtered, having remembered Jenny's nightly mission. His thick tongue did not inhibit the expression of his displeasure.

"Chippy?"

"Yeah, my *wife*," he slurred. "Got all dolled up to go tease other men. So where is she?"

"I'm sorry to inform you, your wife has been in an accident… she didn't make it."

At that point Dunstan completely lost it and had to be sedated. The Police investigation into the suspicious death of Jenny Truman continued without any help from her husband, which may or may not have been to his advantage. The upside was that Dunstan was moved to the psychiatric ward where he received round-the-clock care and was no longer mouthing off and incriminating himself. The downside was that he was not able to explain coherently what had been going on between him and his dear departed wife.

The death of Jenny Truman was the talk of the retirement residence. The excitement, indeed the pleasure, it seemed to give many intrigued the police.
"Did you hear the news?" said one woman to her friend.
"What's that?"
"Jenny's library card *expired* last night."
"Oh, *perish* the thought," rejoined her friend.
"Yes, she must be *mortified*." And the two elderly women broke into gales of laughter over their clever repartee.
Over at the sideboard two more women selected cookies.
"Coshed upside the head they say."
"What a way to be *put down*."
"Oh, Deirdre, you are so clever." They stirred cream into their coffees and took them into the lounge.
Over by the fireplace sat a threesome.
"Now, Daphne. I know you told her to cease and desist but she must have misheard you, because she *de-ceased* and *desisted* instead." The two friends laughed conspiratorially while keeping an eye on Daphne's husband whose response to the news of Jenny's demise was to take it as a personal loss.
He sat there muttering, "What a shame... Such a loss." He raised his eyes heavenward intoning woefully, "We shall miss you, our little coquette."
Over by a sunny window sat a husband and wife. "She expired? Our Jenny Truman expired?"
"Yes, Gregory, and they think her husband did her in."
"Dunstan? Quite impossible! Most definitely and undeniably impossible. He adored his Jenny."
"As did all you warm blooded gents," she glowered.

From the night staff, the police compiled a list of residents who had visited the piano lounge the evening of Jenny's final flirtation. Detective Thorn drew a floor plan and charted the comings and goings of the evening. He sat with it before him as he spoke to witnesses. The interviews went something like this. Detective Thorn would seat the elderly individual or couple across from him and ask, "Can you tell me about last evening?" After some coughing or throat clearing, invariably hesitant voices grew stronger and the telling more animated as they mentioned the woman of the hour, the inimitable Jenny.

"Mrs Bond and I love to while away an evening at the piano. I was playing a love song to my darling." Mrs Bond reached over and fondly patted Mr Bond's hand as he spoke. "We were singing a duet when Jenny arrived." After a thoughtful pause Mr Bond added brightly, "Jenny was delightful, just delightful. Spending time with such an alluring creature always left me feeling young and vigorous."

Thorn noticed Mrs Bond's hand tightened as she sank nails into Mr Bond's tender flesh. Turning to her he asked, "How did you feel about Jenny Truman's flirting?"

"Well, what can I say," she huffed. "Jenny was never selfish with her charms."

"Didn't it bother you to have your private moments interrupted?"

Mrs Bond sat up straight and clasped her hands. "The lounge is a public area. Anyone is free to join in."

"Would everyone join in when the two of you sang?"

"Not if Mr Bond and I were singing to each other. But after a short while we would invite others to sing along."

"Did Jenny observe this custom?"

Mrs Bond began twisting her rings. "Jenny was a non-conformist, a free spirit. A very... free... spirit."

"You seem to stop short of saying what you really think," challenged Detective Thorn.

Mrs Bond inhaled sharply and drew herself straighter. "One must not speak ill of the dead!"

"Tell me Mr Bond, how did Jenny conduct herself last evening?"

"Well, after a while she perched herself upon the piano."

"Yes, you could say she really leaned into the songs," Mrs Bond hissed.

Thorn looked at the photo of the dead woman. "Jenny Truman's attire last evening was, shall we say, very *décolletagée?*"

Mrs Bond clasped her husband's proffered hand and squeezed. As he winced Thorn observed that her rings were now turned round with the sharp stones cutting into the palm of Mr Bond's hand.

"Was it Jenny's habit to flaunt herself?"

Mr Bond flushed pleasurably at the memory, but his wife

started to giggle.

The harder she tried to suppress it the more hysterical she became, until she finally blurted, "She... Jenny... she really has slid off the piano for the last time, hasn't she?"

Mr Bond excused himself and escorted his now hiccupping wife back to their apartment.

Detective Thorn conducted many polite interviews. Try as he might to elicit details, his efforts were thwarted. He called in constable Bastion.

"It seems we are up against it. This generation of witnesses is operating under the maxim, 'One must not speak ill of the dead'. I pose open questions and prod for more details and get what amounts to polite chitchat. However, the body language is very telling. The men were quite enamored of Mrs Jenny Truman. The women are a different story. Whether single or married, they found her flirtatious demeanour quite distasteful, some even given to jesting over her death."

"It's the same in the lounge, sir. The ladies seem almost gleeful as they spread the news, while most of the gents are saddened."

Detective Thorn gave himself a shake and expelled a mock growl. "Only been here a few hours and already we're starting to sound like these octogenarians. Much too polite." He indulged in a few choice expletives just to ground himself. "What's the preliminary report on the blood found on Mr Truman's pajama shirt and other items?

Constable Bastion consulted his iPod. "It's all hers."

"The interviews did not turn up any additional suspects so it's not looking good for Mr Truman. I called the hospital. The psychiatrist thinks we should be able to talk to him later today. Have you located other witnesses?"

Bastion shook his head. "Talked to staff and residents... nada. Asked around if maybe an employee had a grudge against Mrs Truman. They found that funny, said she was one of the more colourful characters, and a good reason to come to work. The front desk doesn't have guests sign in but there is closed-circuit TV on the exits, stairwells and elevators. I'm on my way to visit security now."

"Good. See if they will release last night's recordings to you, or if we need a warrant." Detective Thorn headed to the crime scene.

Jenny Truman's body had been found inside the cloakroom by a departing guest around 11:00 the previous evening. The hallway was taped off, but a few inquisitive residents craned their necks around the corner to watch the detective as he examined the blood stained carpet. Thorn found no sign of struggle and no sign of what had been used to strike the fatal blow to the base of Jenny's pretty little skull.

As Thorn finished his inspection, constable Bastion arrived, triumphantly waving a disc. "Good, you're back. We'll look at that right after the autopsy, which starts," he consulted his watch, "in half an hour."

Detective Thorn was a keen participant, scrutinizing every detail of the autopsy. Fibres found in the wound did not appear to come from the carpet or the victim's clothing, leading to the conclusion that the weapon, the proverbial *blunt instrument*, was wrapped in something.

The coroner noted that the one and only blow, was delivered with great force by someone approximately six feet tall. A tiny laceration on the victim's left ankle was attributed to shaving. "Those can be big bleeders," he added. No alcohol or drugs were present in the victim's system. Fibre samples from the head wound have been sent to the lab for analysis.

Thorn and Bastion headed back to headquarters.

"Let's take a look at the security recordings." The officers identified residents and staff they had already interviewed. "Check the parking entrance camera... Wait. Who's that?"

Constable Bastion leaned in. "The hoody hides the face. Can't tell if it's a man or a tall woman... carrying something heavy in a cloth bag." The person went off camera.

"Did the individual come from the garage or the north stairwell?" Thorn scrolled through other camera angles for the same time period. "Can't be sure. Look at this. Isn't that Mrs Truman?" They watched. Something or someone attracted Jenny's attention and she headed off-camera towards the cloakroom. "That must be when it happened." Thorn stood.

"We'll bring the laptop and security disc with us to the hospital."

It was 3:00 p.m. when the police entered the secure ward. The psychiatrist insisted on being present for the interview. Dunstan Truman was agitated and pacing. The officers noted his height.

"Mr Truman. I'm Detective Thorn and this is Constable Bastion. We found you last night, passed out in your apartment. Do you remember?"

Dunstan stopped pacing and looked from face to face. He seemed to have trouble focusing. The doctor placed a chair behind Dunstan and gently pushed him into it. "What happened to my Jenny?"

"I hoped you could tell us. What do you remember about last night?"

Truman took a long time to answer. "Jenny got all gussied up... again." His lip started twitching.

"Were you going out together?"

Dunstan flushed. In a low voice he said, "Jenny was going to do '*a little harmless flirtation*'. Yeah." He heaved a deep sigh.

"Flirting with other men. Did that make you angry?"

"Yes... well no, but..."

"Well, which is it?"

"Jenny's so young and curvy... I'm... older."

"She was flirting with other men," persisted Thorn. "Not home with you. Did that make you angry?"

Dunstan pressed two fingers to his left eyelid, trying to hold it still.

The detective leaned in. "I think it made you very angry. And the more you thought about it the angrier you got, until finally you went to find Jenny and teach her a lesson."

"No. She didn't need a lesson. She was going to stop."

"But she wasn't stopping soon enough, so you picked up something heavy and..."

"No. No, I never hurt her. Never."

"I think you did, and we have you on closed-circuit television to prove it." Thorn indicated to Bastion to set up the laptop.

The doctor intervened. "Is this really necessary?"

"Listen, Doc. Jenny Truman is dead and the evidence is pointing towards her husband. He's going to have to face it, here or at headquarters. Your choice."

Bastion set the laptop in front of Dunstan Truman and pushed 'play'. As the image of the hooded person came into view Dunstan started swaying and crooning.

"No. Emmeline. No... no... NO!"

The officers looked at each other. "Who's Emmeline?" Thorn held Dunstan's chin, forcing him to make eye contact. "What's her last name?"

Dunstan mouthed something.

"Say it again. What's Emmeline's last name?"

It came out a whisper. "Truman."

"Truman? Is Emmeline Truman a previous wife?"

Thorn now had to hold Dunstan's face with two hands to keep it steady. "Who is Emmeline Truman?"

Dunstan Truman's eyes glazed over as he whispered. "Mummy."

# *A Letter from Mrs Beezie Boddy*
## Neven Humphrey

Some people just want to impose *their* values on others, and they always wind up ruining special events for everybody.

Dear School Wardens,
    This is Mrs Beezie Boddy (I'm the mother of Annie Boddy, in one of your Grade 8 classes) and I am truly disappointed with the outright debauchery going on at this school. It's like, *anything* is permitted over there! So, me and other like-minded parents had put together a series of recommendations. And we expect all of these recommendations to be implemented by the school post-haste, or else we will be pulling our children out of this 'Las Vegas' of an institution.
    First, school should start on the first available school day after New Year's Day. That means either January 2nd, or Monday January 3rd or 4th. One day to celebrate the New Year is enough.
    Valentine's Day should not be celebrated at the school since it's hurtful to the less-popular students. And so any students caught exchanging Valentine's Day cards at the school should be expelled on the spot! And if they're caught kissing they should be forcibly married, and then expelled. Hey, if they want to engage in that sort of activity on school property, why shouldn't they have to face the consequences of it? Finally, teachers or any other school staff engaging in any Valentine's Day activities, be it only making cards in Arts and Crafts class, should be fired on the spot!
    Not everyone is Irish on Saint Patrick's Day, no matter what people say. Thus, Saint Patrick's Day should absolutely not be celebrated at school. In fact, any student caught with anything green on them on Saint Patrick's Day (even if it's just a green pencil, or lettuce in a sandwich) should be sent home, and not be allowed back at school until the 'situation' is rectified. Same with the staff, or face dismissal.
    Now we come to Easter, a Christian holiday. Not everyone at school is Christian. Thus, anyone wearing anything during Lent that's deemed to be promoting Easter must be pelted until

submission with hard-boiled eggs. As well, any teachers participating in Easter activities with their students must be fired on the spot!

Not every child has the luxury of having both a mother and a father, so why should we embarrass them by holding Mother's Day or Father's Day activities at school? Children love their parents already at home; they don't need to be flaunting it at school. Thus, teachers who make students construct Mother's or Father's Day cards or gifts should be fired on the spot!

Now, we come to Hallowe'en, the second-most disgusting holiday of the school year. Not many religions recognize this 'holiday', and even among the Christian faith some groups condemn it. And besides, what's the reasoning of parents sending their child to school dressed up like a ghost or a goblin, when his or her school clothes would be much more appropriate?

We believe that a celebration that mixes black magic with calorie-heavy food should not be allowed at the school. And we demand that a ruling be made that any student going to school on Hallowe'en wearing anything that could even be misconstrued as a costume, i.e. glasses, odd-coloured clothing, casts, crutches, etc. should be told to go home and change or else face expulsion. (They can wear anything they want after school, when they go trick-or-treating.) Now, some students may be forced to wear adaptive devices like glasses to go to school; and students do get injured sometimes, thus the need for casts and crutches. We accept that, but to be able to enter the school, they will have to bring a note from a doctor that says that what may look like a costume actually isn't. And finally, teachers or other staff caught wearing costumes, or engaging in Hallowe'en activities, must be fired immediately!

And now we finally come to the most disgusting celebration of all: Christmas. This Christian celebration has been imposed on the world by force; we have the right to not have it imposed on our school. Thus, anyone caught wearing a red hat, a red coat, black pants or black boots in December will be asked to go back home and change, or face expulsion or dismissal. The same thing goes for anyone who's wearing clothes that look too Christmas-like; e.g. with fir trees as a pattern. As well, anyone caught offering a gift or a card to another person during that same period must be expelled or fired, and their 'generous deed' must be destroyed in the school furnace. (They have plenty of time outside school to exchange gifts and stuff.) Even those simply wishing someone a Merry Christmas should face disciplinary measures. After all, everyone knows the correct greeting is Happy Holidays. And while we're on the subject, school should stop for the holidays only on December 23rd (or the last Friday before the 24th) and start again on the 27th (or the first Monday after the 26th). Our children don't need more holidays than that.

Let's switch to another category now: the school curriculum. We want to examine all the books used to teach our children, and if we find anything in them that might be considered offensive, even if it's just one sentence, we want that book to be removed from the curriculum. We will also be looking through all the books in the school's libraries for any 'offensive' material.

Finally, we want to have a say in all cultural or other events that will happen at the school. And if we don't approve of the event for any reasons, the event must be cancelled. As well, if there is an event organized by the school and involving students, we must be allowed to attend the dress rehearsals. And if we don't approve of something in the event, it must be changed, or else the event will have to be cancelled.

With all my regards.
Mrs Beezie Boddy

# The Writer
## Norm Rosolen

The Writer sits in the back of the squad car, his hands cuffed behind his back. He's very uncomfortable, but he scarcely notices. He's preoccupied with the events of the previous hour.

He's been writing since early morning, when his Wife enters his small attic office and begins pacing the floor behind him. She hurls invective and it appears she has reached the end of her patience when she sweeps the Writer's pens and pencils, collected in a tin cup, to the floor. For added effect, she slaps him on the back of his head.

"Please go," he says. "I've done nothing to deserve this angry outburst. I need to write. It's the source of our livelihood. You constantly interrupt and never allow me the time I need. I feel like I'm in a Kafkaesque prison."

The Writer searches in his mind for an apt description for his Wife's behaviour. *Apoplectic fury? She raged like some kind of, of... Tasmanian Devil? Rabid wolf?* He scribbles in his notebook with a ballpoint pen.

The Writer's Wife is having none of it. "Wake up you stupid old fool. You've insulted me enough and made my life unbearable. And you expect me to shut up. Be your quiet, subservient, doting little plaything do you?"

"Well, when you put it that way..."

"Don't test my patience any further, for you've taken it all. You ignore me, leave me alone for hours. You say you go for long walks, as if I'm to believe you. But I'm no fool. You're seeing someone. I know you. You stare through to the panties of every Pretty-Young-Thing that comes into your view when we walk on the Avenue. From there, it's a small step to a mistress."

The Writer knows better than to disagree for in some remote sense she's right. One time, on such a walk down the Avenue, he stole a glance at a Pretty-Young-Thing and perhaps imagined slightly more than was morally correct. He wished it to be a discreet peek, unnoticed, but his glance was noticed, and the Pretty-Young-Thing cemented his indiscretion into history when she smiled at him and fluttered her eyelashes. The Writer bore his Wife's wrath for two days after that, then in diminishing doses for another week.

"I don't understand what she can see in you other than a pay cheque. You are a terrible lover, and I'm sure your teeny dick…" The Writer's Wife squints at the small gap made between her index finger and thumb. "Your teeny weeny dick is no more satisfying to her than it is to me."

The Writer knows better than to argue, but he attempts a defence. "I must apologize, my dear, for having been born with such a meagre appendage, but my tongue seems to have found its mark enough times." The Writer sticks his tongue out, waggles it and blows a raspberry. A smile momentarily cracks the Writer's Wife's demeanour.

Years ago this would've led to a better outcome, a smile transformed into a laugh and then a kiss and then lovemaking. Their congruent lives would've marched blissfully onward. To what? To this.

Anger restored, his Wife crosses her arms and stares at him menacingly.

"At parties you leave me and talk to others. And why are those others always beautiful women? Have you no shame? I'm always mortified by your prurient behaviour, as are all those women who're subjected to it. On top of that, you torture them with your windbag yakking. Do you know that? You think you're a great writer who captivates everyone with his wit and wisdom but the truth, that you can't fathom, is nobody wants to hear you." The Writer's Wife's voice is pitched slightly below a scream.

The Writer hears sounds through the wall of their abode from the adjoining semidetached house. A family lives on the other side and is no doubt listening through the parchment-thin panel that separates them. He thinks of a description. *Their attention hung on every word.* God no. *Umm. Their ears strained to catch the real life drama.* Hmm, slightly better. He scribbles.

"You would like to see me dead wouldn't you? Poison, a knife, smashed at the bottom of the stairs…" The Writer's Wife's face screws into a hideous mask, and she shakes like a participant in a wild tribal dance preparing for war. He hears murmurings through the wall.

The Writer must leave and go on one of those long walks she abuses him of. He tries to stand, but she pushes him back down. He reckons this venting could go on for hours, and he will take no more. *The Writer was like a poisonous snake trapped in a wicker cage,* he thinks. *Um. Like a cobra. Better. Needing to strike. Okay, okay.*

The Writer decides to get up again, and again his Wife attempts to reseat him. This time he pushes through her and moves to the door. Almost sobbing she says, "You coward. You can't abuse me this way." Then she runs in front of him and beats him with her small, ineffectual fists. He stands half a foot taller and is 80 pounds heavier. He can't be denied.

The Writer desires to go down the stairs. The Writer's Wife takes a great arcing swing at him. The Writer moves back, and the swing carries the Writer's Wife into a tottering semicircle. She pitches down the stairs to the landing, accompanied by a piercing wail.

To the Writer, it seems to occur in slow motion. He sees her utter fear, joined with loathing, as if to say, I'm going to die and do not dare to save me you putrid rat. He sees his notebook on his desk. There is no time for that now.

She lies still, her head twisted grotesquely, eyes motionless, trapped in their glaring hatred. The Writer, of course, has to apply mouth-to-mouth resuscitation. Her lips remain pliant, but they cool as he works. There isn't even a flutter as her soul departs. He's surprised to see water dripping onto his Wife's face, and realizes it's his tears.

The Writer tries to conjure up apt words. *She lay twisted like a pretzel? God no. A crazy wire puzzle? Hmm.* He's too rattled he decides, to give the scene its due.

The bell rings incessantly, and the sound of voices and fists banging on the front entrance intrudes on his concentration. For that's the one thing he can do well. Concentrate. The door gives way, and the police come, followed by their Neighbour's Wife who babbles like an auctioneer while she thrusts an accusing finger at him.

The police pull him aside and take over the artificial respiration. The Writer knows it's to no avail. He hears more sirens. The policeman questions him, quietly, professionally. The Writer answers and knows he's saying too much. Soon the cuffs are applied, and he's led to the cruiser.

A plea of innocence will be protested and mocked. The Writer's Wife's family is well connected and never approved of him. The Writer's Wife and the Neighbour's Wife were friends, and the Neighbour's Wife always frowned when she saw him. He thinks, *My goose is cooked. True cliche.*

He contemplates how long his sentence will be. Probably the rest of his life. He'll have plenty of time to write.

# The Solarium
## Raeanne G. Roy

*D*octor Paisley Johannsen jogged through the streets of the colony. Her colony. The warm amber light shone through the protective dome. Rooftop gardens adorned pod homes with foliage-covered walls as the predominant structures in the settlement. Plants were integral to the way of life here. Without them, proper oxygen exchange was not possible under the dome. Due to solar power's unreliability on Mars, the plants and humans powered the buildings. The colony bustled with activity. A sandy-haired boy and curly-haired blond girl kicked a ball about the basalt stone courtyard.

The year was 2029. Sixteen years ago the Mars simulations had begun in Hawai'i. Those early missions had been much shorter and more specific. The first had lasted three months and focused on diet and nutrition. Subsequent simulations had tested the emotional consequences of living on another planet. With many variables previously accounted for, a mission spanning more than a decade had been deemed necessary. This particular simulation had begun 13 years ago. The researchers realized they needed a group numbering in the tens of thousands to ensure genetic diversity if humans were to truly colonize Mars. Paisley had been selected as the mission's leader and Reese as head of security.

Jeremiah, Reese and Carmella's boy, ran into her as he went for the ball.

"Sorry, Doctor J," he gasped.

"That's all right Jeremiah. Can I assume you've finished your community hours for today?"

"Yes, Doctor J. Amelia and I finished all our work and were told we could go play."

"How are your parents doing?"

"Mom's been a little tired, and dad didn't come home last night."

Odd. Reese's position was largely a formality as life was peaceful here. Weapons were forbidden. A relaxed pace of life that centered on each person having purpose fostered a thriving community. Rita, Amelia's mother, finished tending to the hemp crop and set up the painting supplies she had borrowed from the central lending library. Carmella joined her with other colony members for an informal painting class at no cost. They paused a moment to help another member of the community finish his work, so he would be free to join them. Learning required no money as anything created added to the collective culture of the colony for all to enjoy.

Reese and Carmella had met under the dome four years into the simulation. Before long they were completing each other's sentences and one could scarcely be found without the other. Reese would make up silly reasons for security to be in Carmella's zone. Jeremiah had been born the same year. He had never known anything but dome life.

The mission's end date neared, but six months ago a sickness had hit the colony hard. Paisley, an infectious disease specialist, was baffled by this pathogen. It was unlike any she had studied previously; each time they thought they had the answer, the bug mutated and killed off hundreds. The birth rate could not compensate for the mortality rate imposed by the pathogen. If they did not produce a viable and stable vaccine soon it would mean the end of the outpost.

Paisley reached her office and scanned the landscape beyond the wall-height window where she saw the entire colony from above. She could faintly see her own milk-chocolate freckled skin and ginger curls in the window's reflection. Paisley donned her snow white lab coat, which was made of hemp like so many other textiles in the colony. She entered the adjacent lab where Mica diligently worked on a new version of the vaccine. They did not have the luxury of time to run clinical trials. Nor had they animals to test on. As a result, it was necessary to skip over several quality checks and inject those infected before knowing whether or not it would cure them or condemn them. Paisley fought back a cringe each time as her gut spasm reminded her it was wrong to use humans as lab rats.

In another room, one such patient awaited the shot. They had lost a few earlier in the year to renal and liver failure. Another's eyes liquefied and ran out their sockets, but that could have been the pathogen rather than the vaccine at fault. This particular patient had a treatment before this one and suffered hair loss as a result.

After running the vaccine through the machinery, Paisley could test it on the patient. The woman, Abigail, quietly sat in the cornflower blood drawing chair ready to receive the injection. Her skin had yellowed in the past couple of days. Her voice had grown feeble and was so soft it was barely audible.

"Is it time, Doctor J?"

"Yes, Abigail."

"Will it cure me?"

"We... hope so."

"I guess hope is all there is now."

As Paisley prepared to administer the injection, a lumbering man with dark hair and blue red-rimmed eyes burst through the door.

"Stop what you're doing, Doctor J," he said icily.

Paisley raised her hands and turned to face him. Before she accepted her position as colony leader, she was trained to handle any situation that could arise. Doctor Johannsen calmly engaged Reese in discussion to probe him for information and to gauge his mental state.

"Reese, what can I help you with?"

Sweat dripped from his brow causing him to blink rapidly and repeatedly wipe it with the sleeve of his robin's egg blue uniform. He had a laser pistol pointed at Paisley's heart. Smeared blood adorned his left arm.

"Did you know I was in line to be commander of this station?" There was a maniacal gleam in his eyes. Sweat on his brow. Signs of the sickness.

"What have you done, Reese?"

His laughter filled the room.

"It's imperative they see the mistake they made in appointing you."

The sickness did not cause such anti-Unitarian thoughts. He acted selfishly; his ego could not see the big picture. She tried to appeal to his emotional side while engaging the transformation trigger on her high heels to convert them into flatter footwear.

"What about Carmella?"

"Carmella died last week."

She slowly shifted to one side in an attempt to shield Abigail.

"And Jeremiah?"

"He's sick. He'll be dead soon too."

Reese lied. Paisley had spoken to Jeremiah in the courtyard earlier in the day. He was full of vigour while he kicked the ball around. And did she not see Carmella painting earlier?

"We have a new vaccine. There's no reason he or you have to stay sick."

A fib, but she needed to defuse him with words. The vaccine had not been perfected yet. Some element was missing. What they had developed likely only slowed the progression.

"No! The boy is too sick," he said.

"He told me you didn't go home last night. What were you doing all night?"

"I had to make them see... It's your fault."

"You had to make who see?"

"The watchers. They know and see all."

Reese was too far gone. The sickness had entered his brain stem judging by his behaviour. Paisley could not continue wasting time on this. She dropped down and kicked his legs out from under him, but not before he fired and struck Abigail. His head smashed into the doorway and then the floor. Reese's body slackened and his hand let go of the pistol. After she tucked the pistol in the back of her loose skirt, Paisley checked on Abigail. Her weak pulse and burnt arm needed care Paisley could not provide. She ran to her office and called in the medics who promptly arrived.

While the medics went to work on Abigail, Paisley returned to the lab. The vials of vaccine had been smashed. Refrigeration units were shot up. Her bio-tablet lay in pieces after it had obviously been chucked against a wall. The lab and their work were destroyed. A trail of blood led her to the far corner of the room where Mica slumped. He had lost several pints of blood.

She ran back to the room where the medics worked to stabilize Abigail.

"Come quick," she said.

One followed while the other stayed with Abigail. They did not make it to the lab.

Reese launched himself at her, teeth first. She lifted the pistol but was not fast enough to stop him before he bit her on the arm. The sickness had mutated again.

What was it Abigail had said? Something about hope being all there was. Paisley did not subscribe to that notion. One could sit about hoping things would get better or one could take actions to ensure it would. She had always been the latter type of person.

The medic disinfected and bandaged her arm after she euthanized Reese. There was no other option as he posed too much of a threat in his deranged state. Paisley drew blood from him. She would get the lab back together and begin work on the next vaccine, which she would test on herself.

# Native
## Benoit Chartier

*I* miss you, Vaniel.
It's been a bit more than a cycle since I last held your face in my hands, on that day that you left.
You left.
Two words.
Two tiny words that resonate like thunder within the walls of my mind.
Each day I come to the edge of the enclosure to glimpse you again, but how would I recognize you after your transformation? My hands pressed against what feels like glass, I watch the aliens walk by diffidently, hardly throwing a look in my direction.
A few more young ones have come to the light of day since your sable skin was last against my palm, yet none of them have your crystalline purple eyes, or your sharp and haughty chin.
The youngest play within this terrarium we call home as if they had not a care in the world. Why would they? They never knew the open fields, the endless streams filled with fish, and ocean without bounds.
But you did, didn't you? Is that why you left? To see what they did with them? Or *to* them.
We all have choices to make. Leave, and become alien. One of them. An invader. Stay, and have your memory erased. Forget your past, your roots and your ancestry.
I'm looking through the glass on the edge of the pasture where I used to play as a child. Replaced by a row of grey, lifeless buildings lining a busy street. I'm sitting cross-legged and pondering the creatures I see walking up and down, living their lives. Oblivious to my existence. Oblivious to my pain. To them, I am the alien. The one to look down upon. On my side, grasses held still for lack of wind. The glass wall, three feet thick, 25 feet tall, running straight and smooth for a mile at least, turning 90 degrees, going another mile, doing the same three more times and rejoining this wall. The corners are curved, and offer no purchase. All is slick and smooth and indestructible.

We know.
We tried.
One entrance, or rather, exit only. And we know well what happens to those who depart. Gene replacement therapy to become an 'imperfect' version of the aliens who placed the open-aired glass box over our village, so many moons ago.

That child walking by, sneering with derision, mouthing words, like spitting. I know what he thinks of me. Yet, even if I did as you, Vaniel, I would still be taunted and shunned.

Yet sometimes I come and think I do see you, in a smile or a tress, or the long-legged gait of a particularly beautiful female. Your absence is the equivalent weight of the black hole Korvalis that syphons Ganna Majoris into its blackness while Ganna Minore continues to shine and evade its grasp. And, just like Ganna Majoris, I feel myself growing less and less every day.

It was because of the others, I suspect, that you packed your things that day. I remember it had only been a month since their arrival, but you would tell me every day of your growing unease and anger. Why had they transferred so many of our cousins and far-off neighbours into our tiny village anyhow? Did they not think that our living 20 per dwelling was not excessive, that it would create problems? I'm sure you certainly thought so.

I resolved to make my own lean-to on the edge of the village, but I would often come home to find it torn down. I suspect newcomers were responsible, but I shy away from blaming our kind. Things are difficult enough as it is.

And every night we drink to forget. We drink the golden poison the alien race has bestowed upon us. As if disease, mind-wipe, the theft of our home and land, and the never ending torture of a life without future and hope were not enough, the shashan drives us insane, lustful and violent.

Was it the passing of your sire that cemented your decision? When Elder Grael took his lifespark down the shy path to waiting Vorkalis? Too early, too early. The tears I dried for weeks and months, your hollow cheeks dark pools where smiles went to die.

I could have stopped you.

I should have stopped you. But you are my all, and I would have been a fool to step in the road you've carved to be a wall.

No matter how foolish I think it is. How callous it might be to abandon your kind. Pfa! Beware the torn heart wavering from love, to hate, to disappointment. It drowns itself in seas of pity, but does not search for help.

Tonight I will sleep under the stars while the others gather around the bonfire and take the shashan, fight and rut, trying to forget by circling their own black holes. And I may join them one last time.

I dreamed of you this morning Vaniel, in the moment before I woke. This is not so strange, because I always dream of you. But it was different this time. You did not beckon to me to follow you outside the enclosure, or push me aside this time, unlike before. You stood under my favourite moran tree and gathered long branches. You were building. I remember the suns so bright, brighter than ever I'd felt them before. They tenderly prickled my skin, as they had when I was a boy, running the fields by the village. You looked at me and smiled, and I also gathered branches, and we made sanctuary.

You must think me drink-crazy, but I did not partake last night. I needed to think.

When the lean-to was finished, we went inside and sat in silence. I saw you gathering herbs and potions. I do not know where from; this was a dream. You gave me the resulting concoction, and I drank.

Clarity descended upon me, and I saw all the pieces of all our lives, dancing like leaves caught in a tornado but, at the same time, they were *us*. We would bounce against each other and hurt one another, but still we spun out of control. I saw myself in that tornado, and then I was inside it. Heart wheeling, no up nor down, only careening without end. I glimpsed the ground, though, and aimed for it. It felt so far and impossible to grasp, but then I did, and missed!

What a horrid feeling to rise up again, hitting the others, hearing their shrieks in the maelstrom, but not being able to do anything about it. I gathered all my strength and when the ground returned to me, I planted both my hands, my arms, deep into the soil, and stuck there, swaying like a halu tree.

But I did not let go.

The others saw this and they, too, tried the same. Some hung onto me. Others tried planting themselves firmly into the ground. Those who managed to grab on were saved.

Those who did not, blew away in the storm.

Then it was calm, and we looked at each other and laughed. I cried, I laughed so much. With my hands planted all the way to my elbows in the rich, deep earth, I howled laughter with those who'd held on and stayed with me.

Then I returned to my body. I saw it had been a vision. But I still felt the earth tickling my elbows, its cool embrace around my hands.

You looked at me, smiling. Oh, Vaniel, I could never resist your smile! You know that! I felt a shining within myself that could have erased scars.

I woke up inside my lean-to.

I walked, as I always did, to the glass wall that cut our two worlds in twain like a knife.

One hand on the chill transparency, I observed the denizens of the other side without animosity, longing, or fear. Why would I? I had, with your help, built sanctuary in my heart.

I have to admit, my first urge was to run outside to try find you. You would have laughed, I am sure, to see me in my new skin. I know I could recognize you now, whatever you may look like.

No. I will stay here for a while. Our people are in pain, and I have to show them how to replant their roots, before what is left of them is blown away into nothingness. We owe it to ourselves to live, but not only that; to thrive.

Our culture must live on, in whatever form it takes. What has been forgotten, must be relearned. The roots that have been cut, replanted. There must be pride, and direction and *purpose* for us.

I have no doubt we will make it through, stronger than before. Old Vorkalis will have to wait a while longer for us to travel the shy path into his gaping maw.

I know this because I have hope. Because you never let me give up.

# Thanks for Your Service
## Rem Westland

The major from the National Investigation Service, who had ordered Captain Weatherhill's arrest, had not been to this country before and stayed within the safety of the green zone the whole time he was here. In my view a person should not judge what happened in that Afghan family compound without knowing what it's like in this place.

It was high summer. The land was hot and dry; the dust was always in our mouths, noses and ears. The fields were crisscrossed by ditches, or wadis, that were part of the Afghan irrigation system. The wadis, sometimes many metres down, were lined by earthen walls. The mud at the bottom could be knee deep. It was like campaigning in the middle of an obstacle course.

When on dismounted patrol, carrying 75 kilos of weaponry and gear, we could not use the roads. The roads were where the Taliban planted their improvised explosive devices. When we used pathways along the edges of villages our hearts were in our throats and our breathing was uneven. When on patrol with the Afghan army unit we were mentoring, we were lucky to get even four hours sleep in a day.

We walked looking down at our feet, stepping within the footprint of the one who went before. That way you were less likely to trip an IED. Those devices rip a person and anyone standing close by to pieces. The combined severing of legs, arms, and genitals had become the signature wound in Afghanistan. Medics used the words dismounted complex blast injuries.

Anything suspicious on or under the ground would call for a stop and an inspection. A culvert could be crossed only after one of our unit's Afghan soldiers crawled through to confirm it was clear. The visual presence of fighting-age males, each and every time, demanded a stop in our progress and a confirmation of their intent.

Our last patrol was a 10-day odyssey of unending stops and starts. Each stop was unnerving. Each start filled us with the adrenalin surge that comes with the possibility of ambush. One out of every two times we met fighting-age males they turned out to be Taliban. The Taliban, or Timothy as we called them, would scurry off to pre-set positions and commence firing. We were in a firefight with Timothy every other day.

Incoming rounds register as snaps in the air. You feel them before they can be heard. You learn the difference between a snap and a crack. The sound of a crack means that the bullet has come far too close. When the space around us was filled by snaps and cracks our captain kept his cool. He always got us through.

Our captain had an uncanny ability to sense what was going on around us, even if everyone, including him, had dived behind walls and could no longer see anything at all. Captain Weatherhill knew intuitively what Timothy was doing. He knew where Timothy was likely to pop up next. Our captain would get us advisors and the Afghan soldiers to where the Taliban would be eagerly running, thinking they had us fooled.

The Afghan army was not the only allied Afghan organization in our area. We were at the edge of Pakistan. The border police were the ones we worried about.

It was not unusual to come across those scary guys, fully armed, yet wearing light clothing and perhaps not even shoes. They could look like hippies back in the 1960s and 70s. They were ill-disciplined, often under the influence of drugs, and loud with their voices and their equipment. Small and poorly muffled Hondas were a preferred way for them to scoot from place to place. They took those motorbikes away from Afghan civilians whenever it suited them to do so. I saw this happen on a number of occasions.

After a few months in the field it could be hard for us Canadians to stay positive about the Afghans we were in that country to help. The conduct of the Afghan soldiers we were mentoring could be bizarre as well. We learned not to trust anyone.

When our patrol approached the village of Talukan our attendance at a shura, a meeting with elders, had not been expected. We were unaware of any provincial reconstruction team projects in the vicinity to talk about. We were just passing by. The senior Afghan officer in our unit told us that the meeting would take place in a family compound at the edge of town. For him to refuse, he said, would have been an insult.

We had attended only a couple of council meetings in the whole time we had been embedded with this unit. When something not normal is going to happen in a context where the word normal hardly applies, one moves to the fringe of predictable behaviour.

The captain told us to be on high alert.

The compound looked foreboding.

Its construction was of the thick mud bricks typical in this country. The building was surrounded by walls well over three metres high, with an entry gate facing west and two towers on either end of the southern wall. The compound was large, about 40 metres square. When I peered in I could see a small courtyard with a number of closed doors along the insides of the walls. By my count there were six separate rooms, three built into each of the northern and southern walls. The doors were covered by a metre or so of overhanging tin that ran from one end of each wall to the other.

The open space within the compound allowed only a small group to go inside. The Afghan commander and four of his platoon represented the Afghan contingent. Our team of advisors was represented by Captain Weatherhill, his signaler Master Corporal Brant and the translator Ali. Corporal Kempt, our rifleman, stayed outside with me and the dozen other Afghan troops.

As I stepped back from the gate our captain broke away from an exchange with Brant and pulled me aside. He told me to confirm the coordinates of the compound itself and then, separately, of each of its two towers above the southern wall. He instructed me to then send the coordinates to the British forces on the other side of the Arghandab River.

As the gate was closing, from the southeast came a hard riding group of yahoos. There were 10 of them. They were waving their rifles with a free hand and appeared to be yelling and whooping, but all we could hear was the gathering roar of the motorcycles on which they sat. Their loose clothing and robes fluttered wildly in the shimmering air. Their eyes, when they got close, were maniacal.

I remember Kempt crying out: "God damned border police!" We expected a round of frenetic bargaining to happen between them and the Afghan army soldiers. The border police usually wanted ammo from the army before they would get lost.

When the motorcycles pulled up beside the compound, however, all hell broke loose. Adding to the roar of the engines the riders began firing their weapons into the air. The front gate of the compound opened to a crack and then closed again. In the space of those few seconds the Afghan participants in the shura ran out of the compound and into the fields.

As the gate slammed shut the men we had mistakenly assumed to be border police skidded off their bikes and raced to the northern and southern walls. Rope ladders fell down and the Taliban, for that was who they were, climbed to the top in only a moment. My reflex was to send out a Troops in Contact, or TIC, message on my personal response radio. My rank as warrant officer required me to assume command outside the walls.

Inside the compound the world turned upside down.

Our side had heard the roar of the motorcycles. They saw the village leaders dive out the compound's gate when it had opened for that one instant. They saw, each from his own vantage point, the sudden appearance of men on the top of the opposing walls. Four were visible to Captain Weatherhill's group of three. There were at least six more, three on the top of each tower of the southern wall, visible to the Afghan contingent of five.

The instant our captain appreciated his situation the firing inside the compound began. In the barrage of snaps and cracks from the incoming rounds and in the hundreds of rounds of automatic fire directed to the top of the tower visible to the Afghan soldiers, Captain Weatherhill led his team of three in a dash across the open space between the two walls. Weatherhill had had to physically pull Ali over the exposed open ground. Brant told me angry shouts were exchanged between our captain and the translator.

As he ran, Captain Weatherhill ordered me over his personal radio to direct fire from outside the compound to the Taliban standing on the northern wall. We took them out. Simultaneously, through Sean Brant, our captain called for the Brits to unleash Javelin antitank missiles upon the towers. The Brits had received my TIC message. They were ready.

The firefight was ended by a set of massive explosions when the British missiles hit their respective targets. Each of the two towers along the southern wall was obliterated.

Only one of the Taliban survived the attack. He had been seriously hurt in a fall from the northern wall. We watched him get hauled, without regard for his pain, into custody by an Afghan soldier after the gate reopened. On our side everyone got out alive.

We had not known there were women and children inside the two towers. I don't believe Ali's testimony about that. When we had been cleared by the engineers to walk through the wreckage to gather evidence for a report to higher levels, however, we saw the bodies.

The captain and I counted as many as six children and four women among the dead. Enough remained of the bodies of two of the women to see the fear stamped onto their faces. One of them still held her locked arms around the remains of a child. The other women, the other children, left traces of themselves in the bodies, heads and limbs that were strewn about. Reconstruction by our after-action team of experts would be needed to confirm the actual number of civilians killed.

Yes, the towers had been destroyed on the orders of Captain Weatherhill. Yes, the 10 confirmed deaths of women and children were the direct result of the captain's orders. The captain and I were very aware of this when we stepped through the blood and the gore. I could not look Captain Weatherhill in the eye because my agony could have been read by him as a doubt I did not have.

The captain, in my view, had shown great courage by risking his own life and the lives of his two closest advisors in order to direct fire in a manageable way. As he had always done before, he set things up so that the firefight could be quickly terminated.

When Captain Weatherhill was led away under escort we were surprised. When told he had been ordered back to Canada to be court martialed, we were angry. When HQ in Ottawa said the Taliban attack had been a suicide mission—that allied fire upon women and children had been part of Timothy's plan to embarrass the international force and our captain should have known—we were disgusted.

We learned that a judgement was quickly rendered and that Captain Weatherhill was stripped of his rank. He asked for his release shortly afterwards. Weatherhill was a civilian when, off the deck of his parent's cottage at Sharbot Lake, he hanged himself.

He was in his early 30s. He had been a darned good officer and a friend. He had served his country as best he could.

# Vietnam War Memorial
## Ian Prattis

Gaunt with grief:
Motionless:
Stilled, Silenced:
Cold December day:
Grey and bleak.

        I could not move:
        Stunned:
        Frozen in Time:
        Unbelieving:
        Damn it all!
        Damn!
        It!
        All!

It was not my war
don't you know?
They were not my people
don't you see?
Do I protest too much?

                Name engraved black marble slabs
                rising from the earth
                sear into my soul.
                Burning deep to feel the pain,
                of so many deaths, such futility.
                Ball of fire flames my chest,
                chills the marrow cf my bones.

        Subterranean edifice
        hurts me awake,
        transforms deep memories
        for my own kind.
        Fellow Humans.

Americans,
Vietnamese,
All peoples
caught in the sinister web
of dark and deadly shadows
that lurk in all of us:
Hate, Greed and Power.

        I circle the profanity of war,
        nerve center of our world.
        Grimly aware thought:
        Our world must be transformed:
        Our world must be changed:

                And we must do it.
                Transforming ourselves
                then others in swift urgency.
                Else the memoirs
                of our civilization
                are no more than
                monuments To The Dead.

        Our Dead:
        Yours
        And
        Mine.

## Today I Took Up Running
### Susan Taylor Meehan

*I* leave the house to go for a walk, like I do every day. I lock the door behind me, tuck my keys in my pocket and put on my sunglasses. I make my way down the back garden towards the old elm tree and set off on the bicycle path.

It's a beautiful spring day, not a cloud in the sky. There's a light breeze whispering through the leaves. I feel the sun on my face. I am happy.

I hear steps behind me. I shift slightly to the right and a young woman breezes by, earbuds in her ears and ponytail swinging. She looks like she's flying, running in long, graceful strides. She's barely touching the ground.

Without really thinking about it, I pick up my pace. I go faster and faster until all of a sudden, I'm running. It's awkward at first; it's been a long time since I ran anywhere. But soon, I fall into a rhythm, easy, relaxed, almost floating.

It feels good. Good to stretch my legs, to fill my lungs with air. Good to be free of the fog that is threatening to envelop me. I feel like my old self: sharp, crisp, clear, in control.

Thoughts intrude. My son Donny's voice: "Please, Mum, just think about it. This big house; it's too much now that you're on your own. It's time to downsize."

"I've lived here since you were babies," I tell him. "I'm perfectly capable of managing."

Poor darling, I could always see right through him. He's scared. He's noticed that my memory isn't what it used to be. He thinks I can't live on my own any more.

Then the voice of Sarah, my oldest: "It's so much more obvious now that Dad's gone. He used to cover for her."

I see Artie in the kitchen, making supper. He takes down the sugar bowl for tea and stops for a moment. He pulls something out of it. A hundred dollar bill! I gasp. He just smiles, says it's okay, it's a good hiding place, but I'm going to put it in my wallet now. I go and sit down at the table.

So unexpected, that stroke. He died instantly. How long ago was that? Was there snow on the ground? I don't remember.

Suddenly, I stop.

I don't know where I am. Panic grips me. I see the trees, the bushes, the houses, but they make no sense. Things seem to have lost their third dimension, their depth. The sky curves over me like an overturned bowl. Everything is flat, like a giant mural. Flat, and shiny. And alien.

Where am I? My heart pounds. I can't catch my breath.

Relax. It will come to you. It always does. It just takes time.

I wait. There are no thoughts in my head, just sensations. I hear the birds and feel the breeze whiffle through my hair. I wait some more. I hear my breathing slow and deepen. It doesn't take that long. The third dimension starts filling in. I know where I am now. I'm on the bicycle path.

It's probably time to go back home. I turn around and start running again, and just as I reach my rhythm, I hear it: a baby crying. It sounds like Donny. I'm alert, mobilized. What's wrong? I'd better go see. I veer off the path towards the sound.

I'm in someone's backyard. There are toys and a sandbox. A dog is barking. A woman comes out the back door, carrying a shrieking baby. "Can I help you?" she asks, looking suspicious.

"Sorry!" I shout over the noise. "I heard the baby. I thought something might be wrong."

"It's colic," the woman says. "It makes him scream sometimes."

"Try giving him gripe water," I advise. "That always worked with my babies."

She looks skeptical but nods. "Thanks," she says. She turns. It's obvious she wants me to leave, so I wave and jog back to the path.

I run for a while, enjoying the solid, regular feel of my feet hitting the pavement. I see a smiling woman walking towards me.

"Hi, Jenny," she says. I stop. I don't think I know her, but she seems quite nice. I say Hi.

Then she asks me if I would mind if she took some of the topsoil I had delivered this week. I say no, not at all. Then I realize, it's Margaret from next door. She moved in nearly 25 years ago and we've been friends ever since. We say goodbye and go our separate ways.

Soon, I find my giant elm and leave the path, stopping at the back door with my keys out. It's unlocked. Didn't I lock it when I left? I go in. Donny and Sarah are waiting for me. They ask me where I've been, and I tell them. I say I feel great. They say that's terrific.

They tell me my doctor is suspending my driver's license until I can get my memory problems treated. They've made an appointment for me for tomorrow afternoon. Donny will take me. Don't forget, Mum, he says. I'll call in the morning to remind you. He holds out his hand and I give him my keys. Then they leave.

I go to the window and watch them pull out of the driveway. No license, my darlings? I think. No problem.

I turn and walk through the house, out of the back door and down to the bicycle path. I can go wherever I want, I tell them.

Today, I took up running.

# *Hero*
## Barbara Florio Graham

*I* didn't hear the phone, but my older sister did. She opened her eyes, saw the snow out of her window, and knew it was yet another truck in a ditch somewhere.

Daddy owned the largest rig in Southern Connecticut and the only one with a winch powerful enough to haul a tractor-trailer out of a ditch. I loved The Wrecker, as we affectionately called it, and was always excited when Daddy was called out in the middle of the night. He often brought The Wrecker home instead of driving back to the garage, and that meant I could show it off to my friends on the block, especially the boys who lived around the corner.

An 11-year-old tomboy, it had never dawned on me that my father could be injured or even killed on one of these excursions. This is what he did: backed huge tractor-trailers and army trucks in an out of the nine bays at Carl's Commercial Garage, where he and the other mechanics who called him Boss repaired them.

But this truck wasn't in a ditch. It was hanging, precipitously, over the edge of the bridge across the Connecticut River in Hartford.

He didn't encounter sleet until he was well along the Old Boston Post Road. As he drew closer to the bridge he saw fire trucks and ambulances at both ends of the span. A dozen police cars lined the approaches.

Local residents, hearing all the sirens, had come out to look. Bundled up, only a few brave men were out of their cars, because the wind was biting, laced with tiny pellets of ice.

The Chief of Police was in the car that came to meet him. "Glad you're here."

"What have we got?"

"The trucker is still in the cab. We can't reach him."

"Looks from here like a Freuhof. Did you call Andy?"

"He's on his way. Said to tell you they dropped the load in Springfield, so it's empty."

"I figured that. A full load might have kept it on the bridge."

"What do you need?"

"Sand. Lots of it. And plenty of rope so we don't lose your guys over the edge as they pull him out."

"Can you do it?" Daddy nodded.

The State cops were ready for him. They already had bags of sand, brought in from a construction site. They had used heavy rope to secure the edge of the railing still left intact. They'd also set up a makeshift tent of tarpaulin in the middle of the bridge, where several cops had taken refuge from the pelting ice.

Police cars had been strategically placed with their spotlights focused on the truck.

The Wrecker had been hauling trucks out of ditches and up icy embankments for many years. But this was different. The huge tractor-trailer had crashed completely through the railing, and the cab, with its driver still inside, was hanging precariously over the ice-filled water.

Nobody knew if the driver was conscious. He certainly hadn't acknowledged the presence of the police who waved at him, hoping to reassure him that help was on the way.

Daddy pulled the Wrecker well past the center of the bridge, then gingerly backed it up, a foot at a time, his head out of the window to ensure the cops were spreading the sand where he wanted it.

Finally, he got it into position and lowered the winch. In those days one had to manually attach the winch to the rear axle of the vehicle you were going to tow, so the cops moved the tarp tent as close as they could get it. They were wearing oilskin slickers. Daddy was not.

Securing the winch was just the first step. Now came the delicate maneuvering to pull the trailer further back onto the bridge, slowly enough not to snap the cables or the plate connecting it to the cab. Gradually he turned the wheel of the Wrecker just enough to clear the opposite railing, where most of the sand had been deposited so the Wrecker wouldn't end up off the other side of the bridge.

Nobody remembers exactly how long it took. What they did remember was when the cab was finally back on the edge of the bridge, there was a roar of applause and cheers from all the police and emergency workers, as well as from the crowds gathered on either end to watch.

The driver's eyes were wide open. He was clearly in shock, but apparently uninjured. The ambulance, which had pulled onto the bridge as soon as the Police Chief waved, quickly put the young man on a gurney and sped away. The only access at that point was from the far side, because the wrecker and the Freuhof rig blocked the Post Road end.

Daddy doesn't remember any photographers, and it's likely the reporter didn't even try to reach him, just got the story from police and spectators on the bridge approach.

It took him another 15 minutes to tow the Freuhof off the bridge to a location the police had identified as safe.

He didn't take the Wrecker back to the garage, but parked it in front of the house, where I saw it in the morning. As I was getting ready for school, my mother only said that we should be quiet because Daddy was still sleeping.

By the time I walked home from school the phone had been ringing for more than an hour, as friends and family read the *New Haven Register*.

"Local Mechanic Rescues Driver," said one of the headlines on the front page. The story was brief, with little detail. "Carl Florio, owner of Carl's Commercial Garage on Kimberly Avenue, achieved a daring rescue last night when a tractor-trailer slid off the bridge over the Connecticut River in Hartford in an ice storm. The driver survived the ordeal, and State Police praised Florio for managing to pull the huge rig off the railing."

We didn't see *The Hartford Courant* until the following day, when a reporter from *the Register* brought it to the garage to ask for a follow-up interview.

My father brought the paper home. The entire front page was dominated by the photo of the Wrecker, winch still under the back end of the Freuhof, the cab just inside the missing section of railing. It was pretty dramatic, with cops all around and fuzzy spots in the photo from the glare of the lights.

"Hero Rescues Truck Driver," proclaimed the headline, in type larger than I'd even seen in my 11 years.

Daddy was not pleased. "I'm not a hero," he said, his voice quieter than usual. "This is what I do for a living. It's what the Wrecker does all the time."

"But you saved that driver's life!" I protested.
"Yes, and I've done that before, too. It's part of my job. But my life wasn't in danger, so I'm not a hero."
He put his coffee cup back on the table, got up and motioned to me.
"Come here. Do you know what this is?"
His hand felt rough in mine as he pointed to a framed clipping in the front hall.
"That's about my father," he said, his voice still gentle. "He was a hero."
He handed me the frame, and for the first time I read what was inside. Someone had written 'Hartford Courant, 1925' at the top. It was a photograph of an editorial from that paper, yellow with age.

> *The Heroism of Florio*
>
> *Recently there was laid to rest Giacamo Florio. He went down into a dynamite pit to rescue an unconscious fellow worker who had been overcome by the gases there. He placed a rope around his comrade's waist so he could be drawn to safety.*
>
> *But Florio's heroism cost him his life. He was found dead by the gases at the bottom of that pit which had overcome the one he saved.*
>
> *Thus is the spirit of self-sacrifice often exemplified in our everyday life, but fortunately not often with such tragic results. It is the humble status of this worker that has focused general attention on his brave deed. Florio knew the dangers of going down into that pit, but he was willing to take a chance with his own life in order to save another. The rope that would have saved him he wound around the body of his stricken friend.*

The rest of the editorial pointed out that my grandfather would not have been able to pass the literacy tests currently being considered for immigrants from southern Europe.

The editorial continued:

> *Florio had the one thing alone upon which admission to this land of opportunity should be predicated. He was a faithful, industrious workman. He was brave enough to risk his life to effect*

*a rescue. What more does America want? It is our Florios who have done the hard, rough, dangerous work in building our nation's prosperity, and never in its hour of peril has our country lacked Florios as defenders.*

I would be the first in my family to earn a college degree. My father had gone out to work after completing Grade Six, and, largely self-taught, had built a successful business which had sustained us through the Depression and World War II. He was too old to enlist in the service, but kept convoys of Army trucks on the road.

Doing his job, as always.

I have asked myself many times how I define the word 'hero'. I'm still not sure.

# The Little Drummer
## Robert Barclay

*W*e'd had a long day. What with having to travel all the way to Jerusalem for this damned census, and Mary being nine-months gone and just hanging on. Well, you know the story: we stopped for the night in Bethlehem and the only place we could find was a stable, already occupied with animals and stinking to high heaven. But what do you do? You make the best of things, that's what. And then, no sooner had we shucked off the backpacks and fired up the Coleman stove, the baby starting coming on gang-busters. So before you knew it I was a dad (well, sort of), Mary was a mum, and the Son of God was yelling his little face off. Got Him fed and sorted out eventually, wrapped in some swaddling clothes and in the manger laid.

We were getting really sleepy and peace began to settle, but it was premature. You see, some shepherds who had been abiding in the fields, watching their flocks by night, dropped by to Ooh and Aah. Some Heavenly Host had tipped them off apparently. Finally, they took off and we started to settle down again.

Hopeless.

Just as my eyes were shutting, who should show up but three Wise Men? They'd travelled from the east and were about as wiped as us. So, even though we were totally exhausted, you have to be sociable, don't you? I mean, they'd brought gifts—gold and frankincense and myrrh and all that—and me and Mary had to do the unwrapping, of course. The baby may have been the Son of God, but he was useless with scotch tape and string and paper and whatnot. So we admired the gifts, thanked the wise geezers, gave 'em a drink, and started to bed down yet again. They were no spring chickens, those three, and the journey must have cost them. After all, they'd followed this star of theirs through field and fountain, moor and mountain just to get here, and their timing was bang on, give them that.

Anyway, pretty soon the sheep and the lambs, the cow and the rooster and all the rest had lain down again and shut their eyes. Mary and the baby were already far gone, and the Wise Men were wrapped in their gowns and furs and out to the world. The silence descended. Belshazzar (I think that's who it was) started a gentle snoring, his white beard lifting and descending. I thought he needed his adenoids doing, but he'd have to wait a couple of millennia for that. He made a hypnotic sort of background noise, though, as the night descended, and a peace settled over the stable. I slid slowly into sleep…

Hopeless.

What happened next was absolutely diabolical. I mean, don't get me wrong, we like music as much as anybody else—we'd played Mozart to the fœtus, of course, because just like everybody else we wanted a genius—but percussion? Yes, damned *percussion!* Suddenly we're all wide awake, yelling and shouting, Mary and the baby screaming like demented dervishes, the animals bleating, clucking and mooing, and the Wise Men cursing like drunken sailors and near peeing themselves. Why? Because some cocky little bastard had marched into the stable like he owned the place, beating the holy crap out of a drum! Yes! A bloody great big snare drum; *par-ruppa-pum-pum*! What in the name of the Baby Jesus Christ did he think he was doing? I was up in a flash and turfed the little bugger out into the alley, and pitched his drum after him.

I hope that's the last we'll hear of him!

Jesus!

# Welly
## Norm Rosolen

"Bon Welly, bon cheval." The rotund Field Marshall pats Welly on his neck as if that's supposed to be encouraging. But Welly's not encouraged and he hates that name. Welly is Nappy's joke on some odious British General, but to him it's an insult, another on his long list of grievances.

The climb steepens, and Nappy bends forward as much as his tummy allows. "Oh, Welly, the anticipation, the agony. What has chef Burger prepared for lunch?"

Welly suppresses his incipient anger. *How I would like to run over to that drop and buck him into oblivion,* but he knows better. The scuttlebutt's clear enough. Horses, there had been a few, who complain openly about ferrying the corpulent General end up being 'Put out to pasture', and they all know what that euphemism means. A nip, a balk, a hard bounce is all it takes.

At this altitude the breeze is cool and gusty. Despite that, Welly perspires under his load. He clunks along and snorts deep breaths. Then they stop and Nappy dismounts.

There's barely enough grass for a snack. He presumes the sheep with their stupid little bells have eaten every sapling and shorn every blade of grass to no thicker than the width of a horseshoe. Tinkle, tinkle, tinkle. He hates those bells.

Welly sees movement in the distance and looks across the rolling fields. It's a white horse running free. His heart soars and he lunges towards the apparition. His groom yanks him back and pats him on the neck as if that will make him feel better.

But it's not a horse at all. And it's not running free. It's just a cow eating grass. How many times has he done that? Welly's heart sinks back into its misery.

The Grand Army arrives at Orisson just before lunch, a grimy groom leads Welly to a makeshift paddock, and tethers him to a fence rail. He has hay and water. No oats again.

Welly watches the great Emperor seat himself on his ornate throne, surrounded by an entourage of obsequious generals and lower caste officers, guards, retainers, valets, groomsmen, bat boys, cooks, master chefs and servers. A waiter tucks a napkin under Nappy's fleshy chin.

Nappy's tapas are enough to feed a platoon. The Emperor smacks and savours. "What is this wine? Exquisite."

"Rioja, your Excellency. Our advance troops liberated it just yesterday."

"Not French? Impossible."

"Yes, your Excellency."

Welly snorts. *That waiter's going to the front lines. You can be sure of that. Nappy's going to put on another ten livres with this lunch. I hope he relieves himself before we leave.* Then he reminds himself. *Eat Welly, eat. You'll need all the strength you can muster to carry the grand Emperor Blob over this mountain.*

Welly returns to a dark, dangerous place. *Look at him! Gorging himself. If I could bolt right here I could make it.* But he can't. No running, no freedom and—he looks on the bright side—no sausage factory.

Welly then notices that a groom tethered another horse next to him while he was immersed in thought. He steals some glances and is stunned, caught, like a hedgehog in a trap. It's a lady, regal, beautiful, mesmerizing. He shivers.

"Heh, heh, hello," he says.

"I'm sorry if I'm bothering you," she says.

"No, no, not at all." What a lame retort. When it comes to women, Welly has to hand it to Nappy, who he is sure could woo over the Queen of England if wanted.

They talk, share gossip, and eventually, as these things must go, they nuzzle.

"What's your dearest wish, Welly."

"You first, Belle. What's your deepest, most secret wish?"

Belle looks around, slowly, carefully. "Freedom," she says. "To run as far and as fast as I can."

"Oh, Belle, I've thought about that ever since I was a colt."

"Then let's do it. Break free. Run, live, make babies."

"I'm tethered."

"I know how to untether. I'll undo yours."

Welly glances up occasionally, to watch Nappy tucking into his third course. It doesn't take long, and they're free.

"I'm scared," Belle says.

"Me too. But I'd rather die than carry his Corpulence another league. Soon, they'll open the fence, and we can make a break."

"I love my rider. He's kind and gentle," says Belle. "And not heavy at all."

"They're all jer..." He hears distant gunfire, panicked shouts and sharp retorts from French fusiliers.

"Espagnols, Espagnols!" say the shouters.

"Guerrillas. Spanish guerrillas," says Welly.

"Stupid humans," says Belle.

The closure to the paddock is lowered. "They're coming to saddle us. This is our chance. We need to break for it. Now."

"I... I want to. But I don't think I can. He's coming. There." Welly sees a tall, elegant man jogging behind a groom carrying an ornate saddle. "He needs me Welly. I must stay."

Welly breaks for the opening and bowls over the groom and rider. There are shouts, but he gallops. Freedom trumps love it seems.

After a long run, Welly stops and takes a drink from a puddle and to his astonishment sees a distant horse and rider. Is it Belle and what's-his-name? He doesn't need to think. He is, after all, a horse and decides to act decisively.

As the horse and rider close in, he confirms it's Belle and what's-his-name. Welly snorts and attacks. The rider pulls back on his reins and Belle bucks. The rider pitches off her back and rolls a good distance.

"You have a second chance. Take it."

Belle looks at her rider, struggling to his feet, reaching for his pistol, then back to Welly. "Let's go," she says.

As they run, they touch. There's a gunshot. Welly feels no falter. "You okay?"

"Perfect. I've never felt better in my life."

# Hawai'i: A Different Perspective
## Hazel Johnson

A trip to Hawai'i had been on my bucket list for several years, and now my wish was coming true. Ah, the land of sunshine and beaches!

In February 2013 my husband Byron and I arrive late in the evening at the Lihue airport on Kaua'i, the most northerly of the Hawai'ian Islands. Kaua'i is called the Garden Isle, presumably because of its lush greenery.

Our hotel, the Courtyard Kaua'i at Coconut Beach, is located about seven mile north of the airport on a large lot surrounded by palm trees. The beach is about 60 feet behind the hotel. The area is called Wailua, where you find a small village half a mile or so north of the hotel. We are part of an organized tour, the only Canadians in a group of 28 American seniors.

On our first morning in Hawai'i we awake to overcast skies but pleasant temperatures after a night of steady rain. Looking out our balcony window, I see many lovely palm trees waving in the strong breeze and, far beyond them, the sea is stormy, propelling huge waves to shore.

Later we walk into the wind as far as the village to explore our new surroundings. On our walk we see a fair number of red and black hens with chicks and the occasional elegant rooster. They seem tame and appear to be part of the landscape. We later learn that they are feral chickens and nobody owns them. They are a cross between the red jungle-fowl brought to Kaua'i by the Polynesians who settled here and the domestic chickens brought in later by Captain Cook. They breed everywhere on this island and survive because they have few predators, though some people use them for food.

Our first trip with the tour the following day takes us south of Lihue through dense, emerald foliage and past red and grey rock toward Kauai's south shore. We pass Old Koloa Town, the site of the first sugar plantation in Hawai'i. It dates back to the 1830s. We stop to view the Spouting Horn, a lava tube near the shore that sends a jet of water 50 feet into the air thanks to the pressure of incoming waves, a most intriguing display.

Our next stop is at Poipu Beach Park, a calm, protected beach where folks are swimming and where we eat our lunch. The winds are strong and in some places waves are high; we watch a wind surfer perform skillfully in the very choppy waters. Clouds passing over now bring showers, but they don't last and don't interfere with the tour. We end our day at Allerton Garden where a guide takes us on a long hike through tropical trees offering glimpses of a wide variety of them, as well as flowering shrubs and fruit trees. These are planted strategically with waterfalls, fountains and statues. Species of plants from around the world had been brought to this beautiful park. It is most impressive.

It rained overnight again and the wind was unceasing. We are on the bus before 8:00 a.m. today, and head north to the Hanalei National Wildlife Refuge, Hawai'i's largest seabird sanctuary and home to 5,000 seabirds. Here we see the Kilauea Lighthouse, built in 1909, and still functioning as an important navigational aid to vessels sailing the nearby waters. Occupying more than 200 acres, the Refuge is home to endangered birds like the Layson albatross, red-footed boobies and the Nene goose. We see them feeding in fenced areas, flying overhead or swimming in the ocean. We learn that in 1992 Hurricane Iniki struck hard here causing severe damage to habitat and buildings, and loss of birds. Most repairs have been completed since then. We spend an enjoyable and entertaining morning watching birds.

In the next few days we drive by the green Hanalei Taro fields grown in flooded paddy fields or irrigated land. Taro is a major staple of the Hawai'ian people. We also visit the Grove Farm Homestead Museum, which was originally a sugar plantation. It's a large estate with many buildings situated amid tropical gardens, orchards and rolling lawns. It was turned into a museum in 1978. In addition, we visit the Kaua'i Museum in Lihue. It is loaded with artifacts and brings to life the history of Kauai, including the arrival of Captain Cook in 1778. It is a treasure of the island's heritage and Hawai'i's as well.

On our last day in Kaua'i we head west to Waimea Canyon Lookout, stopping briefly at a coffee plantation where row upon row of coffee plants cover the landscape. A beautiful rainbow appears above the plantation just after a shower. There have been at least half a dozen showers a day, but not every time do we see a lovely rainbow.

After winding up Kokie Road past large ochre outcrops and dense green undergrowth, our bus finally arrives at the Waimea Canyon Lookout. And what a sight! This is the Grand Canyon of the Pacific. It measures 11 miles long, over a mile across, and is close to 360 feet deep. Looking down, we are treated to an amazing sight, a most colourful canyon filled with an array of deep red, purple, rose, orange and rust rocks, boulders, mountain peaks and valleys, interspersed with green forest throughout. Unbelievably dramatic! Though it has just rained and is quite foggy, I can't get enough of the view. And yes, rain was expected, as this is one of the wettest places on earth. This canyon was carved thousands of years ago by floods and rivers, and the lines in the canyon walls depict centuries of volcanic eruptions and lava flows. I am sad when we are beckoned back to the bus as I'd love to spend more time here.

This last evening in Kaua'i is celebrated with a traditional luau, a Hawai'ian 'Spirit of Aloha' celebration the Smith family began offering 50 years ago. It takes place in the beautiful Wailua River Valley where we view a lovely peacock and other birds and animals either fenced in or free to stroll about. And here is where we watch the tradition of roasting a pig, which later forms part of our meal. After the dinner is a performance of excellent music and dance. And so our visit on Kaua'i Island ends.

Big Island Hawai'i is the biggest of the Hawai'ian islands and the second island we visit. We land at Hilo International Airport at 2:30 p.m. and are met by Claudia our hostess, who takes us on a two-mile trip directly to Nani Mau Gardens that houses 22 acres of gorgeous tropical flowers, trees and flourishing plants. Nani Mau means 'forever beautiful', a very just description. After 45 minutes of touring, the rain comes pouring down and prevents us from completing the tour. We are driven to our hotel, the Hilo Hawai'ian Hotel.

On our first morning in Hilo it is still raining intermittently. We have an 8:30 a.m. lecture on the volcanoes and, shortly after, depart for Hawai'i Volcanoes National Park, a half-hour drive away. After stopping briefly at the Kilauea Visitor's Center, we walk for about an hour and a half along the Iliahi Trail and around the open caldera of the Kilauea volcano. Even though the rain never ceases, the walk is intriguing. We walk by large ground cracks and caved areas, steaming vents, hot rocks and sulphur beds. It's almost unbelievable what we encounter; the earth seems alive. And the rain has not dampened our spirits. There are still two active volcanos in this park.

After lunch we return to the Kilauea Visitor Centre to view a film on the Kilauea Caldera, then proceed to the Jaggar Museum. Here we get an amazing view of the caldera sending steam high into the air. It is hard to digest all these unforgettable sights. Our last stop is at the Thurston Lava Tube, which is another incredible phenomenon. It is large enough to walk through, although I walk in only part of the way before returning because I do not want to soak my shoes through. This area is just so full of surprises.

Our second morning here is brighter. The day starts with a lecture at 9:00 a.m. on fish, coral and ocean invertebrates. Then the tour bus takes us to Richardson Beach to view the sea life we discussed, and for a swim if we wish. It is a beautiful location with lava rocks, water and trees, but it's not a great place for swimming because of its rocky beach, although some people do swim anyway. Here we get a wonderful look at a turtle in shallow water, some fish and a whale. Claudia retrieves some sea urchins for us to examine. We eat lunch under a roof during a shower, then continue to the Tsunami Museum where we watch videos about the many earthquakes and tsunamis that have occurred all over the world in the last century.

On our final bus trip we stop at the little town of Pahoa in the Puna District. After lunch we continue on Hawai'i Route 137 to Kalapana, a town most of which was destroyed by lava flows. Eruptions of Kilauea volcano that started in 1959 near the town of Kapaho in the south-east have covered many miles of land with fresh lava. Since 1987 lava pouring into the sea has added 600 acres of land to the Island. In 1990 a thick blanket of lava again entombed the neighboring coastal communities of Kaimu and Kapa'ahu. Walking over this black lava I found it hard to believe that as recently as 1990 there was a town beneath my feet.

This scene is shocking to me; it must have been a horrible nightmare for the folks here at that time. As I gaze around, I see many palm trees sticking out of the lava, which were planted by people hoping to green the area once again. The lava is still actively flowing some distance away. I see the smoke where it continues to flow into the ocean.

Our fifth and sixth days in Hilo are spent, despite occasional showers, visiting the Farmers' Market, the Lyman Museum and the Imilao Astronomy Centre of Hawai'i. All offer a delightful array of items to see and enjoy.

The Hilo Hawai'ian Hotel property is connected to Coconut Island by a bridge that on the last day of our trip Byron and I explore. It's a beautiful island with gardens, bridges and ponds, decoratively accented with lava. It was developed after many homes were destroyed by the tsunami of 1960, which was caused by a huge earthquake in Chili.

We also explore the Lili'uokalani Gardens, which are next door to our hotel. In its 30 acres, there are Hawai'ian and Japanese plants and trees, walkways, pagodas, ponds, streams and bridges. Its gardens are trimmed artistically with lava. It also has many birds and a few mongooses, which resemble squirrels but are bigger. Huge palm and banyan trees enhance the beauty of this enchanting park. We spend most of this beautiful day here; the temperature, about $25^0C$, is probably the warmest since our arrival here. At 4:00 p.m. a taxi takes us to the airport.

I can see now that this wasn't the holiday I had expected. Kauai did not have the warm sunny weather I assumed it would. On the contrary it was very windy with many daily showers; a light jacket was required most days. However, most of the sights and activities were very rewarding. Big Island was a bit warmer and sunnier with fewer showers. Our excursions to Volcano National Park and the Kalapana lava area were unforgettable learning experiences and most rewarding.

It wasn't the Hawai'i I had anticipated. But was I disappointed? Gosh no! I didn't see the touristy beaches and a lot of sun. But I saw some unbelievable sights, learned a lot of history and enjoyed the beautiful flowering plants and trees, and the lush greenery the brochures promised. I was delighted with our journey.

# Dawson's Desert Legacy
## Ian Prattis

*D*awson was a wisdom holder of many traditions, Ojibwa, Hopi, Lakota and the Native American Church. He did have a second name, but preferred Dawson. He was a legendary figure in Central Arizona and left a lasting impression on everyone he met. I have encountered many people at conferences and talks all over North America, and when it emerges that I have spent a considerable amount of time in Central Arizona desert country, I am always asked if I know a man named Dawson. He had met all kinds of people in his capacity as a guide and teacher. Yet his attention and presence never wavered in its intensity as he welcomed all into his orbit of wisdom and patience. I first met him in 1987 on a day-long ethnobotany field trip he offered in the Sonora Desert region of Central Arizona. I was the only person to turn up, yet this did not deter him. He generously extended his knowledge of plants and hidden sources of water in the scrubland of the Sonora Desert. His field trip skirted ancient medicine wheels created centuries ago. He talked about plant cycles within the teachings of the medicine wheel, both for ceremony and healing. His mentorship has always meant a great deal to me, especially his instruction of how to build a medicine wheel.

Dawson was a slender yet muscular man in his 60s, though he seemed much older. His manner was slow and deliberate, gentle but firm, though his light blue eyes carried a steely glint. He loved movies and would always sit in the cinema until the end of the credits, the last person to leave. Eyes closed, he made a point of downloading the full feeling of the film. It was the same with people, animals and the desert. He brought a sense of gentle intensity and intimacy to every relationship. The initial connection from that first field trip and movie experience warmed into a friendship. One evening in Sedona, two years after our initial meeting, I received a call from him. He asked if I would pick him up two hours before dawn the next morning.

"Wear hiking boots," he said.

I drove in the early morning dark to Cornville and found him waiting outside his house. I followed his directions to take various forestry roads leading to a reserve on the northern fringe of the Sonora Desert. After parking we hiked for approximately 30 minutes into the desert through a scrubland trail. It was still dark when he gestured that we should stop. We shared a flask of coffee and the intense silence of the desert, interrupted only by the scurry of small wildlife. In the dark of morning just before dawn, Dawson gestured for me to look in the direction of three large cacti directly in front of us. The sun rose and I could vaguely make out the flowers opening. Then Dawson pointed them out. They were absolutely stunning in their unreal beauty, ranging from yellow to dark violet. We sat there for over an hour, appreciating their beauty, as the morning sun rose.

"You had to see this before you traveled home to Canada," were his only spoken words. The morning heat was suddenly broken by a sudden hail storm. We put our packs over our heads and ran quickly to the shelter of the nearest rocky outcrop. The storm lasted only 10 minutes although the stones were not small, making quite an impact on any unprotected area of the body. Dawson looked at me strangely.

"That sure is some kind of acknowledgement from the past, and it ain't for me. What have you been up to Mister Ian?" Dawson asked.

I just shrugged, as I had no intimations of cause. We walked in silence to where I had parked the car. The hailstones were not to be found beyond a hundred yard perimeter of where we had been sitting.

"Beats the hell out of me, though I reckon you will have some building to do back in Canada," said Dawson cryptically, as he peered at me out of the corner of his eye. These were the last words I heard him speak. As was his custom we drove in silence. He got out of the car by his property, waved once and was gone.

On a later journey in 1992 to that region of Arizona, when enquiring about him, I discovered to my dismay that he had been killed in a car accident outside Phoenix. I was deeply saddened by this loss, thinking about all he had so patiently taught me. I drove to where I had last walked with him, to pay my respects to this extraordinary spiritual teacher, remembering the way almost without thinking. It was not the time for the cacti to flower but I treasured once again the gift he had shown me. I wondered who he had passed on his vast knowledge to, then realized suddenly that he had passed on a great deal to me about medicine wheel lore and construction. Dawson was a spiritual guide and had taken me through many shamanic journeys. The hailstone storm was no longer a mystery to me; rather an early prompt. What I had received from him was put into place in the hermitage where I lived, in the Gatineau Forest in Quebec.

Over a period of five months in the spring and summer of 1994 I experienced very intensive shamanic journeys with an Algonquin shaman that I prepared for through fasting, meditation and sexual abstinence. On five separate journeys I met and dialogued with ancient shamans from the East, the South, the West, the North and finally to the ancient shaman of the Center. I figured at first that this was an experience with five facets of the same archetypal material from my deep unconscious, though there were major surprises I had not anticipated. Each shaman created distinctive unconscious energy within me, interconnected to the other four. In each journey I was always met by the same beautiful female figure, who then led me to the ancient shaman. Dawson had repeatedly told me that the feminine source would eventually emerge as a Muse for me, and there she was.

At my hermitage in the middle of Gatineau Park Forest in Quebec, I had a small circle of large stones in my front yard with beautiful ferns growing at the center. I had an overwhelming compulsion that summer of 1994 to build a medicine wheel with this circle of stones as the interior circle. I had been taught by Dawson the appropriate mind-state and procedure of respect to construct a medicine wheel. Dawson had instructed me intensely in Arizona about the central circle of the medicine wheel. It could only be truly experienced when connection to the sacred mystery was intact. The four cardinal directions East, West, South and North were the organizing axis for this ultimate fusion, re-presented by the ferns over which I took such care. It had sunk into my intellect but now reached my heart.

I constructed the medicine wheel with the assistance of two friends who shared my respect and training. We carried out the appropriate ritual, and worked with reverence on a very hot and humid summer's day. The silence that settled on all three of us spoke of something happening inside and around us while creating this architecture of incredible grace, power and beauty. The stones for the medicine wheel came from my garden and the surrounding forest, the hard granite of the Canadian Shield, part of the very ground where the medicine wheel was being built.

After filling the four quadrants of the medicine wheel with fresh garden soil, we contemplated what had been created. I realized its connection to my five shamanic journeys over the previous year. The cardinal points of the wheel and its center were a reflection of the five ancient shamans I had journeyed to meet and the ferns at the centre were an appropriate symbol for the feminine Muse that delivered me. The medicine wheel was a symbolic map of my internal experience. I was reinventing the wheel from my journeys to meet the five Ancient Shamans, yet also ensured that the beautiful ferns remained intact at the centre of the medicine wheel.

I started to smile at how this medicine lore and knowledge had gradually seeped into my consciousness from Dawson. His overarching influence had prepared me for the journeys to the five shamans. I could feel his intense blue eyes watching me at this moment and perhaps he permitted himself a smile too. It was his instructions I followed for my medicine wheel. He had known that I would eventually understand the wheel and the space at the center as the locale where I would seek counsel from the internal feminine; the beautiful ferns.

# The Message of the Rose
## Peggy Lehmann

For some people, tending to house plants can be more than just a task to keep them alive; it is also one of many activities that instills a sense of calm and a feeling of joy. Making time for moments in life that bring peace is a necessity for balance and wellbeing. It is not relevant how large or small the endeavour; what matters is the experience of timelessness that opens us to our own inner wisdom, from where the greatest inspiration flows. This state can be achieved through reading, gardening, running, painting and other pastimes, and with the stillness of meditation.

To maximize the limited window space my indoor plants have, I purchased a plant stand having four shelves arranged vertically. On the top shelf is a beautiful fern that has already outgrown its original pot, and now its individual stems have extended to dangle carefree over the plant below. Originating from the cactus variety, the unique greenery under the fern has segmented foliage that spreads outward, and is approaching the newest addition under it. My prayer plant is a gift from a friend. When I received the small shoot, it took time to develop its elaborate root system, but once established, it continued to sprout new stems. The haphazard growth of its stems creates a jumbled network of stunning leaves, at times curled slightly and upright, then later open again to face the Lght and display its varying shades of green marked with striking red veins. It is a welcome splash of colour among all the green foliage and cascades almost to the floor, which is in notable contrast to the plant relegated to the bottom shelf and barely visible under the beautiful leaves.

Over two years ago, for my birthday, I was given a miniature rose plant. Its multitude of tiny red flowers dazzled from its four-inch diameter pot. A thoughtful and lovely gift it was, but I knew that once the plentiful blooms had faded I might never see another flower on that plant, given my experience with another one of the same type a few years previously. However, I was determined to do what I could and hope for a more successful result, especially since this one was a gift.

Each time I watered and fed my plants, I also gave water and plant food to the rose. After the initial blooms faded there was some new stem growth, limited to a few inches here and there. Each time I was hopeful that the new stem would produce a flower bud, but it never did. I finally put the half-dead foliage with its blend of green and brown colours on the bottom shelf of the plant stand, where it could still receive light between the leaves hanging over it, but its decaying state would not be easily seen.

Seven months into 2015 I found myself reaching out to support friends and colleagues through personal struggles more often than usual, and also receiving the same in turn from those close to me. Though the events varied in nature, many were unexpected, and there was virtually no break in between. This was becoming a year of changes big and small for many of us.

As I pruned foliage and watered soil one day in late July, I was releasing my mind from processing the email I had received a short time before. The news from my niece was that her mother, my oldest sister, was just diagnosed with cancer. She had been in and out of hospital during the previous two years, having different and unrelated ailments, but she always recovered. Though it was troubling that she was in hospital again—this time undergoing more and varied testing to understand the scope of this latest illness—the expectation of her eventual recovery was still my presumed outcome. Hearing now that she could be seriously ill challenged my assumptions and left me feeling very uneasy. I no longer bothered to part the leaves of the plant above the rose, which allowed better watering access to the rose. Instead, for several weeks, I would now reach down and pour water just inside the edge of the container on the bottom.

My niece gave me the task of informing the rest of the family of the news about our sister, since she did not have the strength to face the barrage of questions that would ensue. Thankfully, I would communicate it by email so all five of my other siblings could be told at once, and gratefully none of them lived close enough to justify a quick visit relaying this information. I was also spared the task of informing our aging mother of this news regarding her first born. That task would be decided among my siblings living in the same vicinity.

Elizabeth was her name at birth, but everyone called her Betty. Her arrival many years ago on Valentine's Day, with its symbolism of hearts and roses and the colour red, perfectly reflects in my mind who she was and what she would become to so many people she knew.

The statistics of her life were pretty ordinary. She married young which was common at that time, raised a daughter and a son with her husband, had one grandson and two granddaughters in later life, and worked during the day in administrative positions.

Her love of music led to a proficiency playing the organ, accordion and piano, and to time in a band as a teenager. Also an accomplished artist, she enjoyed creating with calligraphy, water-colours and oil painting, and she taught students at her art studio. Her landscapes and florals are enjoyed by many people in five countries. Her landscapes and florals are enjoyed by many people in five countries, and she taught students at her art studio.

As the weeks went by, I kept in close contact with my niece, and called my sister when I could to offer support. Since the death of her son, and her divorce from her husband, both 15 years ago, her family was just the two of them and her grandchildren.

With arrangements made to visit my sister at the end of September, I was relaxing at home on the Labour Day weekend. Late Sunday morning I was contacted by my brother who had just visited my sister in hospital and was worried because her condition had deteriorated significantly. We decided I would change my plans and travel the very next day to be with everyone. A rush of emotion went through me and for the first time I recognized the possibility that she might not survive this.

Before I left the next morning, I took time to check on items in the house and to water each of my plants thoroughly, not knowing how long I would be away. As usual, I started with the plant on the top shelf and worked my way to the bottom. When I watered the prayer plant, I noticed the stems were tightly tangled, so I carefully separated the leaves that were intertwined. A glimpse of bright red caught my eye. Although the leaves of the plant had streaks of colour in them I was surprised to see what looked like a red flower bud, since this plant did not have red flowers. My curiosity led me to separate more leaves, and indeed I did find a flower bud with a red flower about to emerge. But the biggest surprise was yet to come as I traced the bright green stem down to the plant on the bottom shelf; the rose plant that had not flowered for over two years had one single stem that grew unnoticed to arm's length and curled slightly under the plant above!

When I examined the contents of the pot on the bottom shelf, the rest of its stunted stems both green and brown remained. Even if it had been dormant during all the time I continued to care for it, and it would have flowered anyway, I couldn't ignore the timing of this particular bloom. My first reaction of confusion changed to disbelief, then to wonder. To me this was extraordinary!

I took a picture, then sent it in a message to a dear friend, explaining my surprise and this plant's history. Her reply came a short time after. Being aware of what was going on in my life then, her observation was simple, but the message was distinct and clear.

Life goes on.

On a beautiful morning in September, eight days after I arrived at her side with the rest of the family, my sister Betty took her last breath and released her spirit from the physical restraints and discomforts of this life. Through the days and rituals that followed, many people shared comments and stories of what Betty meant to them. Even more than her personal achievements, the meaning of her life could be seen through the devotion of her daughter and grandchildren; the lines of people waiting to visit at the hospital; art students, dear friends from years ago; and coworkers of all ages, past and present. We, her siblings, couldn't be more proud of the person she was, and we know she would have been humbled by all the heartfelt tributes.

Life goes on.

In reflection, I recognized further symbolism to the mysterious bloom. Red roses are known as an expression of love, and the flower of choice to be given on Valentine's Day. Life does go on after the death of the physical body, powered by the energy of love.

It is no surprise that following my sister's passing many family members had experiences that were out of the ordinary. Hearts appeared unexpectedly, commanding the attention of a particular family member, from cute coincidences while passing signs and entrances, to a heart-shaped ice formation in the middle of a car windshield while warm air was actively blowing on it from the inside, and it was being scraped on the outside. Her favourite perfume, *Red Door* by Elizabeth Arden, was recognized by family and friends on several occasions when its sudden, distinct scent appeared without logical explanation.

Upon my return home, the rose bud had opened fully and was radiant. One week later it had faded. Not even green stems were visible months later despite continued watering, so it was finally discarded.

Message received.

# Bragging Rights
## Molly O'Connor

Everyone living in the country is quick to point out the ultimate advantages of living away from the bare colourless concrete and toxic fumes of urban life. They can expound on the thrill of being close to nature's beauty, the healthy advantages of breathing quality air, eating homegrown food and drinking well water that has not been stripped of its natural minerals and doused with chemicals. I know, because I preach about everything mentioned here. I am a zealot praising to the heavens all the wonderful attributes and advantages of rural lifestyle. I use every method available to get my message across.

My camera, always at the ready, captures the abundant wild flowers that grow along our road and in our fields. I record textures of bark and rock along with winged, furry and slimy creatures that share my environment. I brag about every aspect of rural life and proudly post confirming photos on my blog. Even on the hottest dogdays of summer I spurn air conditioning as one can always find a cool shady spot beneath a glorious maple tree and inhale deep sweet breaths laced with the smell of fresh mown hay. At day's end, I drift off to sleep filling my lungs with soft night air wafting through my open windows. I don't buy bottled water but always carry thirst quenching liquid from home. To me, it's fair game to lord the advantages of living rural to every sad sack who doesn't have that privilege. I love to exercise my bragging rights. I can insert this message into almost any conversation.

"Did you hear that old Mrs Miller passed yesterday?"

"Yes, and isn't it a shame that she drew her last breath in a hospital in the city deprived of country fresh air?"

I confess, however, that sometimes there are adversities we fail to mention.

A few nights ago, I was choked awake at 2:00 a.m. from a deep sleep. I threw off my sheet and hit the floor in record time. I rushed to the open windows, slammed them shut and powered up the fan. The nauseating, throat burning odour sprayed by some dastardly skunk offended my entire olfactory system and threatened to turn my stomach. Closing the windows didn't help. The smell lingered, gagging me. Realizing that my garden room patio doors were wide open, I tore downstairs to close them. Breathing shallow and swallowing to keep my food down, I hurried through the den toward the back of the house. There I noticed the air quality was decidedly improved, not as pungent as at the front. I dared to take a deep breath, filling my lungs to expel the foul contents in them, before attempting to close off the front of the house where that nasty skunk had sprayed.

Returning to my bedroom, I took the precaution of applying perfumed hand lotion so I could tuck my palms under my nose to mask the putrid smell. It was not entirely successful, something like lilacs and skunk mixed, but non-the-less an improvement. Eventually, I dozed off to waken to slightly better air quality but the wrath of that small black creature with the white stripe still lingered. I had to get on with my day which included a trip to the city.

I was happy to escape to the less offensive fumes of urban life as I set out to do some weekly shopping. A mile down the road the car was freshened by a sweet morning breeze. I breathed deeply and relaxed. There truly is nothing like breathing country air.

Minutes later I punched the power button to close the windows, stopped breathing and stepped on the gas. A local farmer was emptying the contents from his honey wagon over freshly harvested fields. Calling it a honey wagon probably dates me as nowadays farming has become a sophisticated industry using modern methods and equipment. This dairy farm has the latest technologies, one of which is a huge manure pit. There the cows' contributions are liquefied to be sprayed over those freshly cropped fields from a top-of-the-line truck that can deliver the offensive guck to acres and acres in a few short hours. What hasn't changed is the smell. Still holding my breath, I greatly exceeded the speed limit to get beyond that choking stench. This was certainly not a day to brag about living in the country.

Arriving at my favourite grocery store, list in hand, I headed for the automatic doors. Walking through the produce department I noticed perfectly formed cucumbers coated with wax and unblemished tomatoes blushing in pesticides demanding outrageous prices. They taste like sawdust. My day had not started out with the most favourable country experiences but smiling to myself, I knew that when I returned, I'd go out to my garden, pick leafy lettuce, a crisp cucumber, some aromatic herbs and two juicy tomatoes.

And you know what city folks: my salad will have unbeatable flavour; flavour you can't buy in a store. On, yeah, living in the country beats city life by far.

# The White Rose
## Raymond D. Tremblay

Tender and delicate white petals softly hugged each other.
How could I not be reminded of my gorgeous caring mother?
Endless rays of loving from her soul still linger within my heart.

Why did my stunning mom love so much? She was such a sweetheart.
Her dedicated mom taught her to love as she was loved, unconditionally.
I look at the white rose blooming on my balcony and I see my mom's purity.
Touched by her immaculate beauty, my heart is gently inundated with pleasure.
Endearing silent words of filial love spring from my soul towards my dear mother.

Racing thoughts and distractions sought refuge elsewhere. Peace arose from nowhere.
Oh but I knew that my White Rose was the One encouraging me to breathe clean air!
She incessantly radiated and incarnated love only to be freely shared with others.
Each time I admire her boundless beauty, I'm reminded of all loving mothers.

In memory of my mom Rose-Alda Tremblay (L'Heureux)
who passed away in Timmins, Ontario, on August 12th 1968
Written on July 30th 2015

# Egg Thief
## Mary Ellen Kot

*I* was an accident waiting to happen. A pajama-clad woman, wearing her husband's size-12 loafers, on snow-covered ice... how could I not fall?

It should have been a relaxing morning. The only thing on my schedule that Saturday was to go see the movie *Lincoln* with my husband, our friend Sheila and my elderly parents.

Now, a sensible person would have planned to be ready for 11:00 a.m. when Sheila was due to arrive but no, not me. Instead of getting dressed, I decided to rustle up some sandwiches. After all, it was a noon-hour movie. Homemade sandwiches would be a healthy alternative to buttery popcorn.

I put eggs on to boil for egg sandwiches. Downstairs to the freezer I went in search of bread. Hopefully there was some white bread to satisfy my fussy father. Upon thawing I found that what I had thought was a white baguette was actually fancy garlic bread with hunks of garlic embedded in it. I proceeded to extract the cloves, creating polka dot bread.

Having found and discarded the offending garlic, I proceeded to make the sandwiches and put them each in a separate baggie. The idea was to enter the theatre with our lunches hidden in our jacket pockets; a secret picnic at the movies. I had just written Sheila's name on her sandwich bag when Pat read her email to me. She was unable to attend. The day was starting to unravel.

Pat left to go play piano for the Parkinson's choir that he accompanied on Saturday mornings. He would meet us later at the theatre. At 10:20 a.m., with the sandwiches in the fridge, I wondered, "Do I have time to make muffins?" Any rational person would have decided not to. My sensible side told me to go upstairs and get dressed. My impulsive side said, "You can get dressed while the muffins are baking. You can do this if you just hurry!" So off I went, into high stress mode.

I put ingredients on the counter, turned on the oven and then realized I had used all the eggs in the sandwiches. There went that plan. Again, I should have taken this as a sign—silly idea—and gone to get dressed. But no, the crazy part of my brain said, "Nancy probably has eggs." She was our neighbour and we were looking after her house while she was in England for a month. In the previous week we had thawed her frozen hot water pipe with a hair dryer. Surely that was worth two eggs?

I threw on my winter jacket over my housecoat and shoved my feet into Pat's loafers. They were the easiest footwear for this very short trip. As I walked down our driveway to the sidewalk, my sensible brain warned me, "This is sneaky ice, the kind of ice that is there, just waiting to get you, hidden under a layer of snow." We had experienced a weird weather week with rain and temperatures of plus 11 one day, followed by minus 15 the next. Laneways were now skating rinks. That morning the ice was covered by a skiff of fresh snow. I nearly flipped as I made my way to Nancy's door.

Once inside, I was happy to see two eggs waiting for me; mission accomplished! I decided not to bother putting the eggs into a container but to carry them in my hand. After locking the door and checking for mail, I turned to leave.

I can't remember taking even one step away from her door. All I know is that suddenly I was not walking, standing or falling. I was already on the ground and there was this incredible pain shooting through my left ankle; a burning, searing pain that screamed, "This time you have really done it. This time your luck has run out. This is a break or torn ligaments."

I'm not sure how long I lay there; maybe five or six minutes. At the beginning I just knew I could not move. It would be folly to put weight on that foot. I resolved to lie there and wait for some unsuspecting person, whoever came along, to help me hobble back to my door. And so I lay there on the ice.

Funny what goes through your mind at a time like that. Profound thoughts like:

"Well I guess we're not going to that movie."

"I wonder how serious this is?"

"Will I be okay to go ahead with our flight to Florida on Tuesday or will I have ankle surgery? If so, Pat should go ahead with Norah and Avery. No sense in everyone's travel plans going out the window because of my stupidity. I'll stay home by myself

and eat Kraft Dinner and watch TV."
"I wonder who is going to come along?"
"Why am I still in my pajamas at 10:30 a.m.?"
"This is going to be pretty embarrassing if they have to put me on a stretcher."

Suddenly I was aware of liquid in my left hand. Had I cut my hand? Was blood dripping all over my down jacket? I looked at my left hand, still clutching what was left of the eggs, all cracked and broken, yolks and whites dribbling through my fingers. I did my best to fling the sticky mess into the snow and not get it all over my coat. When was someone going to come along? It was Saturday morning. Didn't my neighbours have errands to run? Where were all those dog walkers and joggers when you needed them?

After a while the initial pain seemed to subside so I decided to move. Slowly I got up on all fours. Then, using my good foot first, I stood up and took a tentative step with the injured ankle. The pain was not unbearable so I decided I could go home on my own. Slowly I walked, hobbled and slipped along. Using two feet on each stair I made my way into our house and collapsed on the couch.

I could hop on one foot but there was no possibility of going upstairs to get myself dressed. What to do next? First I had to contact Pat. He had forgotten the cell phone and would soon be leaving the Parkinson's choir to drive to the theatre. I pictured him waiting in front of the theatre, annoyed at our tardiness. Fortunately I was able to reach our son Aaron who said he'd find Pat. Next I called Mom and Dad to cancel our plans. Not wanting to worry them, I tried to downplay my mishap.

In the meantime, as I sat on the couch the pain increased and I knew I should take some Ibuprofen to prevent more swelling. It already looked as if a baseball was growing out of my ankle. How was I going to manage this? Who could I call to fetch the medication and my clothes? Who did I want to see me in pajamas and housecoat? More importantly, who did I want looking into my underwear drawer?

Just then Aaron called to say he had reached Pat, and I realized I could wait the 10 minutes until he got home. Thank goodness for a husband; that person who sees you in all kinds of situations. As soon as he arrived I hit him with my request list: medication, clothes, comb, towel and toothbrush. It was a struggle to get dressed, so he helped with my socks and underwear. Dad dropped off a pair of crutches, which helped immensely. I rewarded him with his egg sandwich. Pat gathered up a bag of supplies to take to the hospital: newspaper, magazines, the egg sandwiches, drinks, purse and icepacks. We were set.

The emergency room was crowded. Every person there had slipped on the ice. All in all, it was a satisfactory experience; we were in and out in two hours, which is amazing, considering I was x-rayed and fitted with an air boot, which enabled me to walk. It was a sprain, not a break. I was advised to do the usual: keep the ankle raised, rest, take anti-inflammatories and wear the air boot when walking. Little did I realize that it would be six months before I would sleep through the night again.

From this totally avoidable mishap I humbly offer some simple life lessons:
- Do not wear men's size-12 shoes, unless they're yours.
- Walk slowly and carefully on ice.
- Get dressed at a decent hour.
- Resist the urge to be busy all the time.
- Relax. Move at a slower pace.
- If you don't have the ingredients, that's a sign you are not meant to make that recipe.
- Enjoy your good health. If nothing hurts, it's a great day.
- Thou shall not steal; not even two lousy eggs.

# There's a Short Story Here
## Robert Barclay

It was too good to miss. Sitting in the window of this little secondhand bookshop on Yonge Street, just a little way south of Bloor, there was the two-volume set of the *Compact Oxford English Dictionary*. It's the one with the magnifying glass in a little drawer at the top. Every single word in the English language, the finest communication tool humanity has yet achieved, there under the lens. Every single word.

He was on a budget; not much editing was coming his way, and even less writing, so this treasure would normally be unaffordable. He reckoned up the asking price in his mind, figuring there would have to be economies; fruit, little treats, bread, they would all have to be cut back. But never, never coffee. Could he really afford it? Could he not afford it? When would he ever see such a bargain again? Could he walk away and leave it there, having only the memory of what might have been? No, the call was too persuasive, the yield so beguiling.

James Murray's *magnum opus* was a damned heavy chunk of paper once you'd paid the price, hefted it into your arms and had begun the trek up Yonge to the subway station at Bloor. By the time he had fumbled out his token, shoved his way clunking through the turnstile, he was slightly regretting the onus in his arms; arms that now felt a great deal longer than they had been this morning.

He entered the subway car and sank thankfully into the first seat that found his bum, the 414,000 words of the great *OED* bearing down upon his lap like a marble sepulchre.

It was at St Clair that she got on the train. She was encumbered like him. Not great tomes of fine print, not long hours of delightful page-turning, not the warmth of classic possession. No; she carried a large square metal cage in which two white rats with shifty, blinky pink eyes scurried and scrabbled. She sank just as thankfully as he across the aisle, the cage across her legs.

You never know when it will happen, but you know it when it has happened. Their eyes met, and that subtle phlogiston that passes between like souls linked them and their burdens together on a higher plane; so much higher than the square, pragmatic steel and plastic interior of a rumbling, moving subway car.

White rats, the great *Oxford English Dictionary*...

There's a short story here, he thought.

# The Year of Not Speaking
## Susan Taylor Meehan

*A*rmand Henry went his own way from the day he was born. If something was popular, he avoided it. If something was despised, he immersed himself in it. His childhood heroes were not athletes or rock musicians. Instead, he idolized Isaac Newton and Stan Lee and Linus Torvalds. He loved science and math, avoided sports and hung out with the other geeks and losers. The popular kids looked down on him and said he had ADD and Aspergers. He didn't care what they thought. He lived in a world of his own, and his world was good.

Armand was an early adopter. When the Internet started to take off in the early 90s, he was already on line. He was communicating with others like himself, first on bulletin boards and in chat rooms, then in more sophisticated online communities and networks. He knew all the programming languages and loved to contribute to open source software. He graduated high school two years early, went to an Ivy League university, and dropped out in second year. But that was okay. He had made a small fortune developing software for games and could pretty much do as he pleased.

He started getting alarmed sometime in the late 1990s as the world geared up for Y2K. Then he saw things get much worse after 9/11. Something was going terribly wrong with the information revolution. It was spiraling 'way out of control. His carefully constructed world was being invaded by video cameras and security cops; unknown parties collected information on him without his consent; he got emails and messages from people he'd never heard of. And there was no safe place: not government data bases, not banks or businesses, not even his own computer.

*Plan A: Hacktivism*
Look, he said to whomever would listen, they have cameras that can take pictures of us from space and we won't even know it. They hear our phone calls, watch our Internet use, catch us on

video as we walk down the street. They have access to all our personal information in every data base everywhere. They know stuff about us that we don't even know ourselves. What're they doing with all that?

Who are 'they'? people would ask. You're just being paranoid. Nobody cares about what websites we visit or what our emails say. And anybody who's afraid of being watched must have something to hide. Just keep changing your password and you'll be fine.

Armand Henry knew everything was not fine.

He found others with similar concerns. They formed communities of interest and became hacktivists. They hacked into high-security sites to prove just how vulnerable they were. They lobbied the IT community for support. They met with government officials and made presentations to legislative committees. They wrote editorials for newspapers and cable TV stations. They spoke at community centres, schools and universities. They stormed the Internet with blogs, town hall discussions and email campaigns.

Only the civil libertarians and social outliers listened. Government officials said security was more important than privacy. The media didn't take them seriously. Politicians wouldn't touch it. The public found it all too complicated and boring.

We have to do something, the hacktivists said. We have to show people how vulnerable they are. Armand brought up the classic sci-fi film *The Day the Earth Stood Still*. We can hack into the power grid, he said. We don't have to hurt anybody, we just have to get their attention.

The hacktivists liked that idea. They set up a huge, complicated plan and on August 14, 2003, they struck. What followed was the biggest power outage in the history of North America. More than 50 million people in the Eastern US Seaboard and Central Canada lost electrical power. Almost immediately, theories began to surface: terrorists; squirrels eating through wires; computer failure; cosmic radiation; Canadians...

The plan was to let the public flounder for about 12 hours, issue a statement, and then restore power. But when they frantically tried to reverse engineer, nothing happened.

Meanwhile, despite the complex precautions the hacktivists had taken, the RCMP's Cyber Crimes unit busted them cold.

*Retribution*
The government issued an announcement that the outage had been caused by a software failure in Ohio. They made no mention of the hacktivists. In fact, there was no way of knowing whether the plotters were responsible for all or even part of the event. But the authorities were not about to play into their hands. The hacktivists had broken the law and they would have to pay.

A core group of six was quietly sentenced to house arrest for five years. They were forbidden to communicate with each other. They were observed 24/7, with cameras in their homes and listening devices on their phones. They were shadowed whenever they went out. Their home computers were confiscated. All their online accounts were closed and saved somewhere in cyberspace for future reference.

They went to work, they came home, they ate and they slept. They watched a lot of television. They worked out in their basements and quarreled with their families. One hacktivist became born again. Another gave up the fight and simply waited out his sentence in silence. One started seeing enemies behind doors and under his bed. He was taken away. Two more became even more militant, convinced of the righteousness of their cause.

But Armand bided his time.

*Plan B: Run Silent, Run Deep*
Eventually, the five years were up. The hacktivists had slowly reintegrated into society. They were impatient to get back on line and catch up with the immense changes that had taken place since early 2004 when they had begun their sentences. Most of them saw the huge increase in IT use as positive. More users leads to more awareness, they reasoned. More awareness means more vigilance.

Armand was not convinced. He saw the mass adoption of social media and hand-held devices as addiction. They've been bought off by bright shiny things, he said. They've all gone over to the dark side and they don't even know it.

On the evening before his release, Armand dined with his parents. He reminded them of his Year of Not Speaking when he was 10, and how he communicated with them about how he felt. He would tape the cover of his latest *Superman* comic to his bedroom door if he was fine, and a drawing of Lex Luthor if he was feeling out of sorts. They asked him if he was okay after five years of house arrest, and he replied that he was feeling super.

The next morning, an RCMP officer came to Armand's apartment, removed the surveillance equipment and returned his computer. "Don't even think about trying anything," he warned Armand. "We'll be watching you."

Armand knew that not all the devices were gone. He smiled his half-smile, thanked the agent, shook his hand, and walked him to the door. Then, sometime before dawn, Armand Henry vanished into thin air.

The Mounties, annoyed they hadn't inserted a microchip into him when they had the chance, were flummoxed. Finger-pointing, recriminations and tougher surveillance protocols followed. Meanwhile, they deemed the disappearance suspicious and launched a massive manhunt. But there was no sign of Armand; no return to his apartment, no visits to friends, no sightings in the city, no record of credit card use, no trail on the Internet.

But there was one sign of life. One morning, his parents noticed that a plain envelope with no return address had been slipped through the mail slot. It contained the cover page of the latest *Superman* comic. There were no useable clues.

The Mounties watched the others in the Core Group closely to see if Armand would try to communicate with them, but no one had seen or heard from him. The member who was born again went to Bible School in Alberta, became a famous preacher and changed many lives. The member who gave up and waited for his sentence to end joined an investment firm on Bay Street and made a lot of money. The member who went over the edge became a recluse and wrote fantasy novels for a huge Internet following. The remaining two lived vicariously through Wikileaks and Anonymous, outwardly leading normal lives.

He's planning some huge event, the authorities said, bigger than the power failure. We need to find him before he does irreparable harm. They put him on the Most Wanted list. They posted his mugshot all over the Internet. They created a hash tag on Twitter and urged everyone to be on the lookout for him. They went on television and spoke to sensation-seeking journalists, hinting that Armand was now working for the Chinese. They spoke at high schools and colleges and community group meetings. They succeeded in making him a celebrity, but they didn't succeed in finding him.

And every month like clockwork, a plain envelope with no return address slipped through the mail slot at his parents' house. And every month, it contained the cover of the latest *Superman* comic.

*Redemption*
The authorities were right to suspect that Armand was up to something. He had found refuge in a safe house run by some members of Anonymous so he could work on a special project: a cloaking device that would enable him to roam the Internet without detection. By his second month of seclusion, he had perfected it. He spent the remainder of his time getting up to speed on the latest developments in communications and IT. And then, exactly one year to the day after he disappeared, Armand Henry resurfaced.

An important meeting was being held at the United Nations in New York. Just as the Chair began to introduce the keynote speaker his microphone went dead, the doors were locked shut and the giant video screen behind him began to flicker. Armand's face appeared before the assembled leaders of the world.

"Good morning, ladies and gentlemen," he said. "I apologize for interrupting your meeting, but I have an important message for you."

Caught unaware, the audience sat in stunned silence. The speaker grabbed his cellphone and attempted to call security. He could not connect. He tried to activate the panic button under the podium. Nothing. Armand pressed on.

"For the last ten years or so, a growing number of IT insiders have been warning the world about the dangers of big data," he said. "Since the early 1990s, we have seen unprecedented growth in the information holdings of governments, corporations, institutions and individuals. But it's been growth without planning, without risk analysis and almost completely without regulation or oversight. It's the Wild West without a sheriff, and today our rights and our liberty are in danger.

"What do I mean? You are all aware of the consequences of unauthorized access to classified government information. But you may not be aware of the consequences of unauthorized access to everyday information. Every time we switch on a light, make a phone call, surf the net, drive through an intersection, buy something, pay our bills—you name it—our actions are counted and the data is stored.

"The trends and patterns found in these statistics help us improve efficiency, reduce costs and develop new products and services. They can help us cure disease, reduce hunger and poverty, promote democracy and human rights. But those same statistics can also be used to disrupt power, transportation and communications; fix the stock market, sporting contests and elections; set prices and reduce consumer choices; the possibilities are endless.

"And worst of all, when combined with our personal information, this data can be used to manipulate perceptions, attitudes and behaviours on a scale unimagined by the advertising industry in the 1950s. Anybody with an agenda to implement, an axe to grind or a product to sell can access and use our data any way they want.

"I, ladies and gentlemen, have that capacity."

He paused and the room started to buzz.

"Soon others will as well," he warned. "The time to act is now! Take charge of this so-called information revolution before it's too late! Make it serve humankind, not subjugate it. You have the power, if you work together."

The screen began to fade.

"I will now return to my place of seclusion," said Armand. "You have your mission. I give you one year to complete it. If you do not, I will shut down the Internet just as I shut down the power grid almost fifteen years ago."

The screen was almost black. Armand's voice was barely audible.

"I'll be watching," he said. "Good luck until we meet again."

# Extras
## Benoit Chartier

*I*'d be far away by the time they realized I wasn't there anymore. I wasn't running away. I'm an adult, and I can do what I want. That's how my parents raised me; to try for the things I can do, no matter how hard it was. This was the hardest things I'd ever tried but, like I say, I had to do it.

I got the official email that Monday morning. Mom opened it for me, after we got our weekly food allotment. It bugged me when she did that, but I guess she did it 'cause she loved me. There was the Interplanetary Exploration official seal on it, slowly turning at the top of the page, so I knew it was legit. Dad kept staring at the thing like it was going to change into something else. I was excited. Looking at Dad and his big round eyes made me laugh out loud, and I covered my mouth.

"Mark! This isn't funny!" he said. I stopped laughing.

"Honey, we have to do something about this," Mom said, like some terrible thing had just crawled out of the flowerbed, and we should call pest control before it spread. I was so happy, though. The letter said I'd been picked! I would be getting onto one of those big transport ships heading out to the new exploration sites of Gliese 581g in the constellation Libra, or Kepler 442b, in Lyra. Me, Mark Spencer, astronaut! I felt my cheeks flush red at the thought of it. This was one of those boyhood dreams that everyone wanted to come true, and it had for me!

"Mark, you're not thinking of going, are you?" Dad said, and I felt a sinking feeling in the pit of my stomach.

"Oh, Mark, I know we said you should always try your best, but this is just impossible! I don't think you're... eligible," Mom said. That was code for: *You can't do it because of your Down's syndrome.*

"I can *too* go! This is the best thing that's ever happened to me!" I cried.

"What about us?" Mom said. "We'll miss you so much. How will we survive without you?" Dad was watching us, arms crossed, and Mom had that sad look on her face that always made me feel bad. I looked at the slowly turning symbol of the Interplanetary Exploration Department one last time and went to my room, without looking at Mom or Dad.

I closed my door and lay on my bed. This wasn't fair. I was 26 years old. I should be allowed to make my own decisions. I had finished High School. I could make my own meals. Why couldn't I join the next expedition?

I leaned over the side of my bed and pulled out my secret tablet from between the mattresses. It was Donny, my older brother, who'd given me the idea. 'Cept his secret tablet had naked lady pictures on it, mostly. Mine was a collection, sure, but they were much nicer pictures.

I flipped it on. The first one was that same logo, the seal I'd just admired on the email. This one didn't move though. It just stayed there. I pressed on it, and inside was a table of contents. I went straight to page 45. That was where the colonizers of Gliese 485 had taken selfies on the tropical planet, and sent back panoramic photos. Big, lush jungles with exotic birds you could only dream of. It looked hot and beautiful. Carey Somerhill, the lead scientist for the expedition, smiled on one of the pictures. Her hair was all mussed up, and the corners of her eyes crinkled with joy. I had met her when I was just young, when she'd come to my school. She was a really nice lady. Maybe that's when I decided I wanted to be an astronaut, too.

I sighed and put my tablet back under the mattress. I put my hands behind my head and looked up at the plastic stars on the ceiling. They glowed in the dark. It was cool. Mom and Dad had helped me put them in the patterns of all the different constellations. I looked up at Lyra, and I was on the ship with thousands of other extras, for the long dark trip through the stars, to find new homes.

Extras is a funny word. That's what my brother Donny calls them. Anybody born after the second child in a family is considered a Supplemental. They're automatically entered into the Planetary Lottery System, and if you're picked, then you have to go. There's only one way to avoid it, and I hoped that no one would come out and take my place. Believe me, a lot of people do, and unless you are an 'extra', or a scientist, then you can't. It's that easy.

Mom explained to me that there's a balance, like a scale, and the entire Earth hangs in it. If there's too many people, then everybody dies. That's what she said. That's why they pick hundreds of thousands of people every year to leave for other parts of the Milky Way, so that there won't be too many on Earth. Anyone born after the second baby: boom, you're on the list.

My teachers told me my parents were brave for having me. I'm not sure why, but I'm sure glad they did. There aren't many people in the 26th century with an extra chromosome. I guess that makes me special. As far as I know, no one with an extra chromosome has gone into space either, so that makes me even more special. So I had to go!

The next day, Donny came over. He lived downtown in a condo. He didn't usually come over unless it was for supper. He was here early. Like, breakfast-time early. It was weird.

"Hey Mark. I have some good news for you," he said. I looked at him, not knowing what to expect. He eyed me nervously. He sat down at the kitchen table where I was having breakfast.

Mom and Dad were standing behind him. Dad had his hand on Donny's shoulder, and Mom had her arm around Dad's waist. I felt awkward, with a mouthful of cereal I wasn't sure what to do with.

"You don't have to go on that colonizing trip. I'm taking your place," Donny said. I spat out my cereal.

"What?" I said.

"Yeah, Mom and Dad told me about it, and I agreed to go for you. You know, it's super dangerous out there. We're just afraid you'd get..." he said, but I cut him off:

"It's my decision! You can't do this!" I felt the tears welling in my eyes, but I ran out of the door before they could see any of them hit the ground. I was mad. I ran down the block, the solar sidewalk giving a faint 'ting' sound every time I hit a charging pressure switch.

I ran all the way to my favourite park and found the old swing set. I'd lived here all my life, and had been surrounded by love all my life. That wasn't the problem. I wanted to be a grown-up now, and this was my chance. It felt horrible to have my family try to take that away from me. I called Kat, my older sister. I knew today was her day off anyway, and she showed up an hour later with her four-year-old son Joey. While Joey played on the structures, Kat and I swung lazily.

"What happened?" she asked, eyeing my sour mood. This is why I loved her. She went straight to the point.

I told her everything that'd happened since yesterday.

"That's tough. When are you leaving?" she said.

"I can't. Donny's going to go for me. He gave his name instead of mine." She turned her face up to the sky, her mouth a thin line. I knew this was her thinking pose. The air smelled of fresh-cut grass, and a little wind blew through my sister's hair.

Joey climbed to the top of the monkey bars and waved with a "look Mommy, I did it" gesture. Kat waved back, smiling.

"You're first in line, though. That's the rule. So do it," she said, with her hand on my back. "I'll take care of Mom and Dad. You do what you have to do to be happy."

So yeah, I snuck out. I'm not proud of that. Kat got some stuff for me, and I gave her a letter to give to our parents. I took an earlier shuttle, and Donny's name got deleted from the rolls. Here's what I told them in my goodbye letter:

*Dear Mom, Dad, Donny and Kat,*

*I'm a man now. I want to live my life the way I want to. You're wonderful people, and you've always been there for me, all my life, but now it's time for me to make it on my own. I've always wanted to do this, and no one can stop me. I know you're scared for me. Don't be. You raised me to be independent, and this is my biggest test. I want you to know how much it means to me that you were always there for me when I needed you. You're the best parents a guy can have.*

*Donny, I'm sorry you don't get to go, but it was me who was picked, not you. I know you wanted to go, and Mom and Dad convinced you to, but it wasn't right, and you know it. I hope you forgive me.*

*Kat, you've always given me good advice, and I love you forever.*

*I will send you all pictures when I get to Kepler 442b.*

*Your loving son and brother,*

*Mark Spencer.*

As I write this, we're several light-years from the Earth, and I'm making new friends.

# Eleanor Does Not Camp!
## Susan A. Jennings

Counting the days to freedom, Eleanor was excited to be out of the corporate rat race. At first, shopping during working hours gave her a thrill; playing hooky incited her to spend money on stuff she didn't need, useless stuff. Her pension, although adequate, did not stretch as far as a working salary. *I didn't think that through too well,* she thought, pushing the large glass doors of Bayshore Mall. She glanced at the mall clock: 11:30. She was early for lunch with Trudy, so she had time to browse. She sighed. *What am I doing? I hate shopping. I hardly know Trudy and what was that all about at coffee this morning?* A light bulb popped in her head. She was bored; coffee and lunching with retired friends who were equally as bored as Eleanor was driving her to screaming point. She pulled her phone from her purse and dialed.

"Trudy, I am so sorry for such late notice but something has come up and I have to cancel lunch." She quickly hit 'end', thankful for voicemail, and ran to her car giggling. She had made a decision and things were going to change.

Five minutes later she unlocked her apartment door, opened her laptop and scrolled through the emails. "Writers retreat," she said aloud. Her fingers tapped the keyboard as she filled in the registration forms and hit 'send'. She waited, staring at the screen, and then it arrived. Confirmed. She sent a communal email to the family, packed a suitcase and pressed the vacation reply button on her email.

The route was simple, Highways 417 and 17 to Renfrew and then 60 to Arowhon Pines Resort. It felt like Christmas; the kid in her, excited at opening her stocking, today's gift a week at a country resort, pursuing her writing, inspired by nature. She would be in the middle of Algonquin Park, not camping, a natural assumption given the location. Eleanor does not camp, nothing less than four or five star accommodation, comfy beds, fluffy pillows, en suite bathrooms and maid service. It was expensive—at least expensive for her—but better than spending on 'stuff' from the mall. She slid a Dave Brubeck jazz collection into the

CD player, set the cruise control to 85, a touch over the speed limit and settled back to enjoy three and a half hours of the prettiest countryside in Ontario. It was a perfect opportunity to change her mindset, and embark on the career of her choice, as novelist. She liked the sound of the word. "Novelist," she said. She sensed some doubt, not about her ability or her decision; another kind of doubt. A dark shadow hovered at her shoulder her intuition quivered. Something was amiss.

"Really, Eleanor, your silly intuitions are playing havoc with your mind. Ignore them," she said aloud. "I am a novelist!" She laughed, humming to Brubeck as she turned onto Highway 60.

The directions she had printed from the Arowhon Pines website read: eight kilometers from Highway 60 on rough dirt road into the resort. *They weren't kidding*, she thought as the car bounced and shuddered over washboard gravel. The sign read Speed Limit 40 km. She looked at her speedometer: 20 km. She laughed; *If anyone tried 40 their teeth would fall out.* The road was wide so an oncoming car didn't bother her, until she realized the massive cloud of dust indicated its speed. It suddenly stopped dead. She slowed to a crawl, coming to a halt just as a moose appeared through the trees and walked towards her car. *Wow! That's a little disconcerting*, she thought. Her reaction was ambiguous; thankful the enormous animal had turned and disappeared back into the forest, yet sorry the glimpse was so short. The car opposite spun its wheels in the gravel, swerving and almost hitting Eleanor as it sped off in a cloud of dust. She caught a glimpse of an angry male face that sent shivers down her spine.

She watched the road carefully for moose lingering between road and forest. Her first sighting was a fitting welcome to Arowhon Pines Resort, but the car encounter hadn't felt so welcoming. It felt sinister. She slowed down, noticing a gap between the trees and the way the dust had cleared at that exact place; the ditch shallow enough to drive a car across. *Is that where the car came from? Unlikely*, she thought. *More likely a city person, not used to the dirt road. So why is every cell in my body sensing danger?* She took a breath to ease the tightness in her stomach. Her car had come to a complete halt. She didn't remember braking.

Her better judgment told her to continue to the resort, but instead she felt her hand on the car door handle and before she could stop herself she was walking into the clearing. Primal hairs stood up on the back of her neck, her heart pounded in her chest, the only sound her own heart beat thumping in her ears. There was a strange silence; no bird song, screaming blue jays or rustling leaves. She jumped as a lone chipmunk darted in front of her; she felt its anxiety as it disappeared into a hole.

The clearing began to narrow into a path, wide enough for one person, definitely not room enough for a car. The ground was dry and hard with no tire tracks, but the grass and brush had been flattened in places. Someone had driven and parked a car here. Logic told her to turn around and go back but her feet had grown roots and she couldn't move. She was meant to stay, but why?

Eleanor sat on a large shaded rock. The sun was hot in the clearing and she was thirsty and tired. She stared at the narrow path leading further into the forest. Holding her breath she closed her eyes and dared not move. Someone was sitting next to her. She waited for the attack; nothing happened, she opened her eyes. A shadow sat on the rock; a man, but his features were vague. He was dressed as a woodsman with flecks of something on his clothes. She remembered reading that the artist Tom Thomson's ghost was known to roam the park. *Could this be him?* After all, Arowhon Pines was not far from Canoe Lake, where Thomson's body had been found.

She felt the danger disappear, to be replaced by a sense of sadness and pain; someone needed help. He pointed to the pathway and nodded. She felt reassured and taking a deep breath she crossed the clearing and walked onto the path. It felt cool after the hot sun. The trees rustled at her side as he was guiding her and protecting her. She stopped mid-stride as he jumped in front of her, gesturing to follow. She followed this vague outline whose steps flattened the brush and moved the branches. *I'm following the invisible man,* she thought. She pinched her arm. *Ouch that hurt, so I'm not dreaming.* He stopped suddenly and she walked right through him and found a young woman lying in the brush, barely alive. Eleanor brushed the blonde hair from the woman's face and gasped at the deep purple bruises on her neck. She gently eased her down to a sitting position and loosened her clothes, remembering Girl Guides first aid. The woman's lips began to move and she opened her eyes. "Thirsty," she rasped.

Eleanor realized she had brought nothing with her. She felt her cell phone in her jeans. Thank goodness. Oh no! No bars. Of course, the park had only spotty service and Arowhon Pines was not one of those spots. "I'm sorry, I have no water," she said, sitting beside the woman. "What's your name?"

"Brianna. My throat hurts. He tried to kill me." She sobbed, tears falling down her cheeks, hand on her neck. She had begun to shiver. *She's in shock,* Eleanor thought desperately trying to figure out what to do. The Girl Guide answer was a warm blanket and hot sweet tea, neither of which she had here in the wilderness. Her own body was all she had for heat. Eleanor wrapped her arms around the woman for warm and comfort to ease the sobbing.

"It's okay, Brianna, you're safe now," Eleanor said in her calmest soothing voice, while her insides were in a panic. She would hardly call their situation safe. No water, food or shelter in the middle of Algonquin Park, bear country, with wolves and other predators. She glanced at the sky; the sun was deep in the west, still above the trees. She glanced at her wrist but she'd forgotten her watch, so she pulled her cellphone out. Nothing; the battery was dead She guessed the time was around five or six, so it would be dark in a couple of hours. First they needed water, but she hadn't seen any streams or lakes on her way in here. Brianna stirred and sat up.

"Are you feeling better?"

"Yes, my throat is so dry."

"Brianna, can you stay here while I see if I can find some water?" She patted her jeans. "But I need something to put it in."

"Here." Brianna pulled a Ziploc bag from her jeans, "It had cookies in it."

Eleanor took the bag and headed into the forest not sure which direction to go. Suddenly she felt his presence. "Tom, you came back. Where can I find water?" The shadowy presence walked in front of her and within minutes she heard running water; a few yards away a crystal-clear stream bubbled over rocks. She bent down scooping the water into her hands and gulping it as fast as she could, splashing her face, sucking up more water. It felt so good. Having drunk her fill she filled the plastic bag and followed Tom back to Brianna. She noted the route so she could find her way back if necessary.

Brianna looked pale, her eyes swollen and her face covered in black fly bites. Some of the bleeding Eleanor thought had come from the trauma was in fact insect bites. Eleanor held the plastic bag to Brianna's mouth and she slurped the water greedily, spilling it on her chest. "Oh, that feels good," she said rubbing the wetness around her neck. Eleanor pinched her fingers along the Ziploc to save the rest of the water. Brianna stood up, shakily and winced as she tried to walk. Her ankle was thick with swelling but she managed to take a couple of steps.

"Do you think you can walk out of here? It will be dark soon and we have no shelter."

Brianna winced again. "I can try. My ankle really hurts. Maybe I could find a stick to take some weight."

"Good idea." Eleanor quickly found a sturdy stick. Measuring it against Brianna, she snapped the top off and handed it to her. Brianna hobbled and tried hopping on one leg. She nodded and said, "This will do just fine. I can walk with the stick."

"Great. My car is up by the road. I think I can find our way back." Eleanor sounded far more confident than she felt; once in the clearing they'd be fine, but the narrow path was hard to follow. She looked around for Tom's shadow, but she sensed he had moved on.

Walking in single file, Eleanor led the way on the assumption she knew where she was going. The canopy was thicker than she remembered and the fading light was making it difficult to see. She heard Brianna stumble a couple of times but kept going because they had to get out of the forest before dark. She turned to see her companion's face white, her lips parted and dry. She attempted to lick them.

"Here you need water." Eleanor handed her the half empty plastic bag. "Let's rest a minute." She glanced around, feeling lost as everywhere looked the same. She couldn't even be sure they were walking in the right direction. The sun had disappeared leaving a red glow on the horizon, and in minutes it would be dark. "Can you walk a little further, we're nearly there," she lied.

"I can't. I'm going to pass out." Eleanor watched Brianna slide down a tree trunk and crumple into a ball." She splashed water on her face. "Brianna wake up." Close to tears Eleanor was afraid Brianna would die.

"I'm okay. I need to rest." Brianna tried to smile.

"Okay, let's rest a while." Eleanor slid down the tree and sat beside Brianna and they wrapped their arms around each other. The sun had gone and they were plunged into the cool forest darkness. At first it was silent then twigs snapped and leaves rustled as the forest night came alive. Eleanor felt the fear and panic in both of them. *This would never do*, she thought. *They needed to stay awake and be alert.*

"Brianna, I never asked you what happened. Who attacked you?"

"Believe it or not, my boyfriend, Mark. We've been dating for about a month. He has a mean streak but until a few days ago I never knew how violent he was. I should have seen it coming. Last week he was mad with Molly my little dog, and kicked her so hard I had to take her to the vet. He said he was sorry and I believed him. Today's trip was supposed to be a treat; lunch at Arowhon Pines. He pulled the car off the road and started fooling around. I wasn't in the mood. We decided to go for a walk and that was when he tried to force himself on me. I screamed and he flew into a rage."

Eleanor could feel Brianna's tears spill onto her bare arm. "He grabbed me by the neck and I thought I was dead. Suddenly he let go. I heard him say, 'Oh, my God, what have I done' and he ran off. I don't remember much more until you arrived." She relaxed and looked at Eleanor, the full moon shining on their faces. "How did you find me?"

"I saw him drive like a maniac on the gravel road, and I can't explain it but I was guided to the clearing." She paused, deciding whether or not to mention Tom Thomson's ghost. "And I just started walking into the forest. I had no idea why, it was very…" They both froze as the unmistakable howl of a wolf broke into their conversation.

Brianna pointed through the trees. Three pairs of eyes fixed in their direction. Eleanor had just opened her mouth to scream when she felt a presence at her side. She turned. Tom was more visible now; he wore a smock covered in paint and was carrying a canoe paddle in one hand, while with the other he placed his finger to his lips. She arrested the scream. She saw him approach the wolves, and they whimpered and the eyes disappeared. Tom sat beside them and they drifted into sleep.

Twittering birds woke them at dawn. Dogs were barking not far away. "Someone must be out for a morning walk," said Eleanor, standing up. "Help! Help! Over here!" she yelled.

A voice replied, "Stay where you are. We will come to you."

Two German Shepherds came through the brush with policemen attached to their leashes, followed by the park ranger and several other people, wanting to help with the search. Eleanor wanted to kiss their feet.

Brianna was carried to the clearing where an ambulance and several police cars were parked. The police bombarded her with questions about her injuries and who was responsible. The paramedics also examined Eleanor and said she was free to go.

The park ranger approached Eleanor. "What were you doing in there at night?" His voice had an edge of exasperation.

Eleanor told him her story leaving out the real hero, Tom Thomson. "How did you find us?"

"An employee from Arowhon passed your car in the early evening, and when it was still there when he came back at eleven he reported it to us. We're always looking out for unregistered campers."

Eleanor laughed, "Oh, I don't camp." Then she thought, *I guess I did last night.*

"I drove out to check your car and called the police to trace your number plate. Arowhon confirmed you were a guest but had not checked in. We took a look around but it was too dark to start a search party. The tracker dogs found you at dawn." He gave her a stern look. "You were lucky. There are wolves and bears out there. I heard wolves last night but it was strange, they only howled once and then went quiet. It is unwise to venture off the trails."

"You're right, I should have known better. But I sensed someone was in danger." Eleanor decided not to say any more as she watched the ranger raise his eyebrows. "I won't do that again and thank you for finding us."

A pleasant young man riding a golf cart was waiting for Eleanor in the Arowhon parking lot. "Are we ever happy to see you! It sounds as though you have had quite an ordeal. Name's Peter. Your bags in the trunk?"

She nodded. The enormity of the situation suddenly hit her. She leaned on the car feeling nauseous and lightheaded.

"Here hop on," he patted the passenger seat. "I'll take you to reception. Terry is waiting for you. We'll have you in your room in no time."

The Arowhon kitchen was coming to life at six in the morning. Someone handed her a good strong coffee and a pastry. The coffee warmed her and she gobbled the pastry, hot out of the oven, realizing she hadn't eaten since breakfast the day before.

The young man Peter took her in the golf cart to her five-star cabin. Her bags had already been delivered to the room.

She stood under the hot shower in her en suite bathroom, dried off and crawled into bed, pulling the duvet up to her chin and letting her head fall into the soft pillow. Her eyes stayed open long enough to capture the view, the peace and tranquility of Little Joe Lake, nature's final lullaby orchestrated by the calls of the loon and the songbird's morning chorus. Arowhon Pines, Algonquin Park at its best.

Eleanor does not camp!

# Biographies of the Contributors

Alfaro, Silvia
  Silvia is the director of Art and Literature, Mapalé & Publishing Inc., an independent publishing house founded in 2004. She studied architecture and worked in the field for 10 years, in the private sector and the Federal Government in Ottawa. She now dedicates her time and knowledge to promoting writers, visual artists, musicians and others through art magazines, books, exhibitions, concerts and literary events.

Barclay, Robert
  Bob is author of three novels (*Triple Take*, *Death at the Podium* and *Ask Me About My Bombshells*) and a range of technical books in the field of musical instrument studies. He runs a small publishing company concentrating on the works of senior citizens and people with mental health issues. His present project is a historical novel set in the Thirty Years War in 17th century Germany.

Chartier, Benoit
  Benoit Chartier is a resident of the National Capital Region, on the Quebec side. He lives with his wife and son, and an overflowing imagination.

Clarke, Jessica
  Jessica was raised in Montreal by an English father and a French mother. Grief at the tender age of 13 prompted her to write, but she soon discovered a passion for the written word, which has only grown with time. She writes strong female characters faced with all too human emotions and situations that leave no one indifferent. She loves to delve into the basest of human nature and draw forth the most exciting or poignant, thrilling or depraved facets of her characters.

Florio Graham, Barbara
  Author of *Five Fast Steps to Better Writing* (20th anniversary edition), *Five Fast Steps to Low-Cost Publicity*, and the award-winning *Mewsings/Musings*, Barbara Florio Graham is a

publishing consultant and marketing strategist who offers mentoring, contract review, and online courses.

Galay, Gladys
Gladys is a Canadian writer with a murderous bent. After a career as a public servant, she is becoming known for her murder mystery stories. Gladys received 3rd prize from Capital Crime Writers (CCW) for the 2015 Short Story Contest and an honourable mention from the NYC Midnight 2016 Short Story contest. Gladys is currently working on two novels; a young adult espionage novel and an adult fiction novel inspired by events from the past.

Ghanem, Qais
Since retirement from medicine, Qais Ghanem has written *From Left to Right*, a book of Arabic and English poems; *My Arab Spring my Canada*, a book advocating total integration into Canadian society; and three novels about Yemeni society: *Final Flight from Sanaa*, *Two Boys from Aden College* and *Forbidden Love in the Land of Sheba*.

Humphrey, Nevin
Neven was born in St-Malachie, Québec. Soon after birth his left eye was removed due to cancer, while his right eye was diagnosed with acute myopia. He has a BA in History (1994). He completed his first novel *To Save a Wolf* in 2005. Since then he has published five other books, including a book of opinion pieces entitled *Tales of Conscience*. (He is currently working on *Tales of Conscience*, Part 2.)

Jennings, Susan A.
Susan is the author of *The Blue Pendant*, a trans-Atlantic saga; a novella *Ruins in Silk*, a story of tragedy and triumph; a memoir *Save Some for Me*, a story of a single mother; and several collections of short stories and cozy mysteries. She is the founder of The Ottawa Story Spinners, and a regular contributor to the *Black Lake Chronicles vol. 1-5*, eclectic collections of short stories. Her next release is *The New Sackville Hotel*.

Johnson, Hazel
Hazel is the author of two books, *RV-ING and Other Adventures North of 60* and *My Roots from Prairie Pioneers*. She has also published articles in local papers, the *Ottawa Citizen*

Biographies

and *Fifty-Five Plus*, and in the online news source *True North Perspective*. She has also contributed articles to past OIW Anthologies. Her other interest is making pottery.

Kafai, Majid (Abdol)
Majid has a degree in Law and served as a diplomat for Iran from 1955 to 1980 in Geneva, Kabul, Vienna, Moscow, Milan, Rome, Ottawa and Paris. He was a Refugee Judge in Canada from 1984 to 1999. Majid is the author of several books in Persian, English and French, and had a show of his paintings in Paris. He was awarded the title of Poetry Ambassador by the US International Library of Poetry and the Poetry Ambassador Program in 2006 and 2007. More than 780 of his poems are on his Facebook page.

Kot, Mary Ellen
Mary Ellen's work has appeared in *The Toronto Star*, *Ottawa Citizen*, *Ottawa Sun*, *The Globe and Mail* and *Chicken Soup for the Soul: Christmas in Canada*. She is currently working on a book of humourous vacation mishaps.

Lehmann, Peggy
Peggy is a writer with a focus on spirituality. Her inspiration often comes through insights in her work as an energy healer, medium and teacher. She is working on her first book about the deeper meaning of our everyday lives, which is not yet titled.

Newton, Keith
With several dozen more-or-less academic articles and books behind him, Keith Newton's publications record dwindled when he retired and tried writing fiction: five short stories, a satirical essay and a wee poem so far. The opportunity to contribute to the current anthology has encouraged him. Onwards!

O'Connor, Molly
Molly is a very active senior who spends her time writing, walking, singing and capturing photos of wild flowers when she is not dabbling in politics. Her work appears in five of the *Chicken Soup for the Soul* anthologies and several other publications. She has self-published four books: *Fourteen Cups* (a collection of short stories), *Wandering Backward* (a

creative memoir), *Snow Business* (a children's picture book) and *When Secrets Become Lies* (a novel).

Prattis, Ian

Dr. Prattis is a Professor Emeritus at Carleton University and award winning author of 14 books. Recent awards include Gold for fiction at the 2015 Florida Book Festival, 2015 Quill Award from *Focus on Women Magazine* and Silver for *Conservation* from the 2014 Living Now Literary Awards. His poetry, memoirs, fiction, articles, blogs and podcasts appear in a wide range of venues.

Rosolen, Norm

Norm's a crotchety senior citizen who hammers away at some short stories and a dystopian novel about how women take over the world. He's been writing for the last six or seven years and has two short stories selected for the *CommuterLit* online magazine and a non-fiction article for *True North Perspectives* web site. Needless to say, he'll take any positive reinforcement he can get.

Roy, Raeanne G.

Raeanne is a Canadian fiction author. She is a passionate martial artist, hobbyist musician and lover of geeky things. Originally from North Bay, Ontario, the youngest of three children, she now resides in Ottawa. She has been writing stories since age nine. She writes in a variety of genres including science fiction, fantasy, romance, erotica and historical fiction. Many of her stories feature strong female protagonists.

Stewart, Laurie

Laurie is the author of two young adult novels and a series of cookbooks. She has published several short fantasy stories, most set in the worlds created for her science fiction/fantasy novels. She is currently working on one novel of each of her worlds: *Dark Fey Universe* and *The Terreagles Tapestry*.

Taylor, Maggie

Maggie is an Ottawa playwright who has written and directed three Murder Mystery Dinner Plays. Her stories have twice been shortlisted for the Audrey Jessop Award from Capital Crime Writers Short Story Contest. Some of

Maggie's poetry can be found in *Cutting the Keys*, a University of Ottawa publication. She is currently writing her 4th play for production in May 2017.

Taylor Meehan, Susan

A native of Edmonton, Alberta, Susan Taylor Meehan grew up as an Air Force brat, living in Canada, the US and Europe. She spent most of her working life as a writer and editor with the former Canadian International Development Agency. Since retirement, she has spread her wings to include a wide range of genres, including historical fiction, short stories, biography and poetry. Her novel, *Maggie's Choice*, is set in World War I and reflects the experiences of her great-aunt, who served as a frontline nurse in Boulogne, France.

Tremblay, Raymond

Raymond, retired social worker as of 2014, is the author of one novel, *Riding the Tides of Life*, numerous collections of poetry and three biographies. A manuscript, *In Search Of New Adventures*, aimed at a children's readership, is scheduled for publication by the end of this year.

Westland, Remmelt

After careers in Canada's military, public service, and consulting, Rem's writing began with a non-fiction account of his run for public office, *Running for the People?*, published in 2015. His first novel, from which the story *Thanks for Your Service* was drawn, will soon be published. His current project is a novel about the impact of the global economy on a small community in one of Canada's eastern provinces.